# The Fighting Marshal

## The Saga of Will Howard

By

Jack D. Coombe

Order this book online at www.trafford.com
or email orders@trafford.com

Most Trafford titles are also available at major online book retailers.

The Temptation-Derailing the Tokyo Express-Thunder Along the Mississippi-Gunfire
Around the Gilf-Gunsmoke Over the Atlantic -When Radio Was King

Printed in the United States of America.

ISBN: 978-1-4269-3921-1 (sc)
ISBN: 978-1-4269-3922-8 (hc)
ISBN: 978-1-4269-3923-5 (e)

Library of Congress Control Number:  2010912719

*Trafford rev. 02/24/2011*

 www.trafford.com

**North America & international**
toll-free: 1 888 232 4444 (USA & Canada)
phone: 250 383 6864 ✦ fax: 812 355 4082

# Acknowledgements

In ant endeavor, such as this book, there are many people who, in one day or another, contribute to its creation. Be that as it may, there some who contribute immeasurably. Included among these are Henry Kingwill who always stood ready to explain some of the techniques of the martial arts. Emerick Lemar who demonstrated some important moves, my fellow author John Glavin who gave immeasurable encouragement. Most importantly, I am most grateful to Mark V. Pierotti who guided me through much of the electronics so necessary for my computer work. My gratitude to Greg Fye for his invaluable help in the realm of photography. Finally, many thanks to Craig Ferguson for always being available to help out in so many ways in this electronic age.

# DEDICATION

To Peg Coombe, my wife, the most important critic and best friend without whom I couldn't produce a dang, worthwhile thing.

# CHAPTER 1
## (Dodge City, KA 1878)

"Going on my rounds," U.S. Marshal Will Howard put on his white Stetson and left his office on Front Street.

He turned and started up the wooden sidewalk, nodding at the men and touching the brim of his hat at the ladies. His tall frame moved with cat-like ease. He was clad in matching blue jeans and shirt. A Colt with white grips rested in a new leather holster at his right side. His mustache revealed a flick of gray.

Will's overall appearance was one of a man who was cocksure of himself and he moved as one greatly assured of it.

"Good morning, Marshal. "Looks like we'll have a fine day," Chalk Beeson, approached and nodded at him.

"Going to open the Long Branch, I assume." Will smiled back at the famous saloon keeper.

"Yep, another day and another day of toil I always say," Beeson returned the smile, a fleck of egg appeared on his big salt-and-pepper mustache.

"Just make sure the day is quiet and without any interruption, Mr. Beeson. I don't like going to your place and hauling off recalcitrant patrons."

Chalk gave a puzzled, but positive, nod the lawman's words.

"Rest assured I'll do just that, Marshal," Chalk replied. He turned and headed down the street, muttering to himself: "A body should have a dictionary at hand when talking to that man."

Will continued up the street, past George Hoover's liquor and cigar store, his eyes taking in everything familiar. He stopped before Wright and Rath's General Store and, after hesitating for a minute and glancing around, he turned and entered. The store was partly empty with a few customers milling around, examining the merchandise.

"Marshal Howard, how are you this fine, spring day?" Robert Paulson, peering through wire-rimmed spectacles, nodded his slightly bald head at the lawman.

"I'm all fine, Bob." Will returned. "How about you?

"Well, I'm keeping one jump ahead of the sheriff," Bob replied, laughing at his little joke. "I suspect you wish to see Margaret. Just a moment. I'll call her out."

He turned and pushed through a large curtain suspended from the ceiling which obviously led into a backroom of the store. Will took a moment to glance around, noting everything; the piles of clothes on a counter and many suspended on wooden hangers from clothes trees. He smiled at the amount of merchandise available, knowing that, as Dodge's only general store, it would soon be full of more items for the ladies of Dodge City.

"Nice of you to drop in," Margaret Howard had appeared, her lovely face beaming with pleasure. "Is everything all right, dear?"

"Yes, Margie, all is right," Will quickly took in the woman of his heart standing before him with her tall, straight frame, topped with jet-black hair elegantly coiffured and her dark eyes focused firmly on him. "I bless the day I first met you."

"You always know how to say the right things, Will Howard. At first I erroneously thought that giving up the ministry would change your perspective on things. But that was a mistake."

"I know that," Will replied. "I don't miss some aspects of being a minister, but overall what I'm doing is supplying a the physical needs of the community instead of the spiritual."

He shifted nervously on his feet, as if the discussion was creating a mixture of contradictory affects on him. "But that's not what I wanted to talk to you about. Are you still planning to come to the picnic at the grove tomorrow?"

Margaret looked closely at him, ostensibly trying to divine his thoughts. "Yes. Are you planning to go?

Will laughed. "Of course. I'll be there with three hats on; one as a father, one as citizen and the other as a lawman keeping order. You know that, Margie. It's a matter of having a new root, even in the same ground as other roots."

She sighed softly. The fear had gone from her. "By now I know in the deepest regions of my heart you mean what you say"

"Yes. Make book on it," Will was smiling broadly now. "I guess that for a moment thought you had second thoughts about our relationship, but now I know better."

For a brief moment he fought down a desire to take his wife in his arms and kiss her. Every time he was in her presence, he wanted to do just that. His love for her seemed to grow as the days passed. It seemed to be much stronger of late.

"Good," she said. "Lucy, Father and the good congregation of the church have invited us to the annual picnic."

"I'm grateful the old animosities have passed since I was pastor there," Will's face grew serious and he wanted to change the conversation. "I must be on my rounds. See you at nine."

He touched the tip of his hat and departed without another word. Margaret stood, looking after him, her mind whirling with a variety of mixed emotions and thoughts. "Oh, Will," she said softly, "I know tings will work out for good for us "

She turned and left through the door curtains.

Will continued his way up the sidewalk, glancing at store fronts and alley entrances, nodding at passerby's.

"Glad to see you're on the job, Marshal," a man said as he walked by. For a while I thought we'd lose you."

"No worry about that," Will replied, smiling.

"Marshal! Marshal! Wait up!"

Will turned to spot his tall, lanky deputy Mark Williams running down the street waving a paper in his hands.

Slightly out of breath, Mark came up to him. "Marshal, I didn't want to interrupt your rounds, but this is important."

"That's all right, Mark. What is it?"

"This note was left at the office. It was dropped in the door, while I was in the privy."

"Let me see it," Will said, accepting the paper.

"I had to read it," Mark said, guardedly. "Sorry."

"That's fine," Will answered. "You thought it was for you."

"Yes, yes, I did," Mark said, visibly relaxing a bit.

Will took the paper and scanned it. It was in rough scribbling, but was eligible enough to read: "Marshal, watch your back at the picnic."

"What does it mean?" Mark asked.

"Obvious," Will replied, "Either he's planning a bushwhacking or he's calling me out."

"Sounds to me more like a bushwhacking," Mark offered.

"Either way, I've been warned, Mark."

"Want me along? I kin' get Slate Nevins to stand in for me at the jail house

"It's all right, Mark. "I'll handle whatever he hands out. Must continue my rounds and see you back at my office."

Will stuffed the note carefully in his pocket and continued up the sidewalk. Mark watched him go: "I'm sure you will, Marshal, but I'd give a month's pay to see you handle that yahoo ."

The next day dawned bright and clear with the Kansas sky deep blue and dotted with small puffs of cumulous clouds. The cottonwood grove on Rattler Creek was alive with early summer finery and the happy chirpings of birds.

As Will rode up his Black and white pony, "Pal" named after the breed "palomino," the grove was already filling up with Dodge citizens. Rows of tables were covered with blue and white oilcloths over which were plates of fried chicken, bowls of potato salad and all the traditional ingredients of picnics.

Will hitched Pal to one of the hitching posts put up by citizens of Dodge. He dismounted and walked toward the nearest group. The group was presided over by Margaret who was clad in a western riding habit and a soft pink Stetson. He face lit up when she spotted Will coming toward her. She went to him and hugged him, unashamedly, while the men and women present watched with amused interest. "Tommy playing with his friends. Don't worry. He won't miss lunch, not a growing boy."

"Good," Marharet replied. "He's like his father. loves picnics."   She leaned back, looked him over, noticing the Colt at his right side. "You wore your pistol?"

Will smiled. "Rules say a lawman to wear his rig whenever in public. You know that. Can't break the rules, can I?"

She smiled broadly. "Of course not," she replied.

Will studied her face to determine of she had any inkling of the warning note he had received. He detected none and for a brief moment felt a flush of shame for deceiving her. But then he realized that the main reason he was armed was to protect her and others from harm.

At this moment, in the corner of the picnic area, a group of musicians consisting of guitar, fiddle and string bass struck up a number and the air was filled with festive music.

"Save a dance for me," he said to Margaret.

"You'd better believe it," she replied with a wink.

At this point a woman came up. "Margie, don't want to bother you, but you're needed at the food table. I'll be with you and Tommy a little later."

"Sure thing," she replied, as she walked over to a vantage point, in order to study the growing crowd of people, looking for someone who didn't seem to belong there.

Will was standing a bit apart from the crowds, when Arthur Love came over to him. "Will. Got a minute?"

"Sure, Arthur. What's on your mind?"

"Word has it you've been called out by a gunman." Is that true?

Fighting down a modicum of anger over an apparent leakage of official information, Will replied, "I don't know who told you and I won't ask. But Arthur, you know I'm capable of handling something like that. Besides I have men nearby, in case of trouble."

Will then made a mental note to get to the bottom of the leak. "Now go about and enjoy the festivities. I don't want anyone getting suspicious and causing a riot."

Arthur breathed a sigh of relief. "Of course. Might've known you'd have everything in hand. Sorry, Will."

Arthur glanced down, spotted the Colt and nodded . "I'll stay close to Margaret and Tommy and keep an eye on them."

He unconsciously patted his vest. Will knew he kept a Derringer in there, as most bankers did and were usually winked at by lawmen.

"Just don't interfere, Arthur," Will continued. "I'll take care of all contingencies."

As Will walked away, Arthur smiled to himself assuredly, as he reassuringly patted the hidden Derringer.

"It's all right, Will," he said to himself. I remember the way you put away that Rye Wilson gang of cutthroats. Margaret and Tommy are safe."

Will went to the food tables found Margaret dishing out pork and beans. "Could I have this dance, Margie?"

She beamed. "Of course." She spoke to a woman next to her, "Lucy, will you take over?"

"Sure," Lucy McMillan winked at her. "You lucky thing."

On the wooden dance floor rigged up by carpenter members of Dodge's citizenry, Will and Margaret began dancing. After a few minutes enjoying each other's company, Margaret said, "Will, I hear rumors of a gunman warning coming after you. Is it true?"

Will sighed. Damn it, he thought, rumors flow fast in Dodge, but who could have leaked the information? "Don't worry about it, Margie. I have a man planted in the crowd. We have everything under control."

Margie nodded her agreement.

"Of course. Now let's forget that and enjoy the day," Will said, holder her closer to himself. He felt a rush of something in his body, a mixed feeling of love and sexuality for holding her close to himself aware of the impropriety of such a normal reaction, even for a married man. Margaret showed no negative reaction.

Suddenly the music stopped and the crowd began to mutter its protest. Then Mark came over to Will. "Sorry, Marshal. We have trouble up ahead."

"What is it?"

"Three yahoos crashed the party and are holding a group at gunpoint. One's asking for you."

"Will, be careful, " Margaret said.

Will turned to some men nearby, "I'll handle this. Watch Marie and Tommy."

"Sure, Marshal," they replied. "If you need help, just call."

"Thanks." Will turned to Mark. "Stay here. I'll handle this. They just want me and no one else need to get hurt."

"All the same, I wait for your nod and I'll come a-runnin' there to help out if need.," Mark's face has creased with a frown of worry

He walked firmly past a quieted orchestra and some citizens. When he reached the edge of the crowd three armed men were holding everyone at bay. One of them, a tall, rough-looking individual spotted Will. "Well, Marshal, what took you so long?"

"Who are you and what do you want?"

"You know what we want."

"No, I don't. Just who the hell are you and what are you doing here? Speak up or get out."

To bystanders it was obvious Will was toying dangerously with the gunman. Mark and some men had come up. "Need us, Marshal?" Mark asked.

"No Mark, this is personal. Just between him and me."

Will faced the gunman squarely. "Once more who are you and what do you want?"

The gunman flashed a cruel smile. "You. I'm Teague Beeson; These are my men, Dolf and Bob. You shot my brother Ham, remember?"

"Yes I do," Will nodded. "He was a bank robber and gutless killer. He got what he well deserved, Beeson"

"You tracked him down and shot him in cold blood," said Cal. "I aim to avenge that here and now." He glanced at the deputies behind Will. "This is between us, Marshal. Make them keep heir guns holstered. We'll settle this here and now. After we kill you, and your deputies, we'll hold up the bank and you won't be there to stop us. Call off the deputies. This is betwixed you and me."

Will nodded at the deputies. "Do as he says. Move off."

"But Marshal--" Mark appeared worried as he turned to them "You heard him, men."

The lawmen reluctantly backed off, leaving Will alone to face the intruders.

"There's a lot of talk here," Dolf said to his companions. "What we waitin' fer?"

"Take him!" shouted Teague, as he went for his gun

'Damn you, Howard!"

Suddenly, Will's hand moved with blinding speed and the Colt was in his hand, firing. Teague was thrown back as the one-ounce lead slug slammed into him.

"Wha--? Dolf muttered. He drew. Too late. Will fired.

The bullet thudded into Dolf's chest, sending him to the ground where he lay with the others, their dead eyes staring skyward.

Then Bob drew and fired. His shot went over Will's head. He took aim to fire again, but Will was once again too fast. His bullet slammed into the gunman's chest. He screamed as he was literally thrown to the ground where he lay spread-eagled.

It was all over. The three gunman were on the ground as Will stood watching them, lest one of them stirred or tried to draw. None did. All three were dead. Satisfied, Will holstered his Colt and faced the others who stood there open-mouthed and unable to talk.

"I've never seen anything like it. The man's greased lightnin'" one bystander said.

"Another Wyatt Earp's here," another man offered.

Then a badly shaken Margaret ran to Will, throwing her arms around him. "I was so frightened." You could have been killed."

He hugged her, patted her back. "Never fear for me, Margie. I'll go to heaven some day but not with a gun in my hand."

He motioned to Mark. "Get Tom Hansom and have him come and pick up this vermin."

Will, you faced them alone. Why?"

"Because it was my fight and I didn't want to put my deputies in danger. It was a personal thing." Will replied, holstering his gun.

Mesmerized, the others stood, staring at Will.

""I'll be damned," proclaimed one man.

"Beats all--" commented another.

Margaret, realizing the understandable sight she presented, straightened and started to wipe her eyes, "I was frightened for you. You were outnumbered three to one by those gunman You could've been killed."

Then Tommy rushed up, threw his arms around his father. "I'm glad your alright, Dad." Together, Margaret observed, they were twin-like, each tall with blond, curly hair and a fine complexion

One man came to Will and said: "You used your gun, instead of your fists, Marshal."

"I know," Will replied. But when facing three armed men, fists aren't fast enough. Guns are."

Satisfied with the answer, the man nodded and moved off.

Will turned to the crowd standing there watching the dead gunman being carried off to the edge of the grove, out of sight and to be picked up by the undertaker and his men.

"Everybody, please continue with the picnic!" he motioned to the band. "Strike up a tune and let's get started."

The musicians did and people started going back to the positions they held before the gunfight began and began dancing.

Will glanced at Margaret. "Know what. I'm hungry. Didn't get a chance to dig in before the trouble started Any food left?"

"I'll fix a plate for you," she replied.

Will winked. "I didn't lose my appetite Let's eat."

They sat with Tommy and Margaret who made sure their plates were full of fried chicken, mashed potatoes and salad. She was puzzled over how Will could kill three men and still eat.

Margaret concluded that that was one thing she'd never understand about lawmen, heir insensibility to death and violence.

They'd been chatting for a time when Will suddenly sat upright: "By gobs, I forgot something."

"What's that?"

"To go for a walk while this wonderful food settles in our innards. Tommy, how about you?"

"No, dad you go. I'll stay with my friends."

Will said, "Alright, son. It's a beautiful day and the grove will be the right place to settle all that food. Come, Margie. Let's enjoy nature's gifts."

Will turned to Mark. "Take over and keep watch on things. Mrs. Howard and I are going for a walk."

Mark smiled knowingly. "Sure thing, Marshal."

Will and Margaret began their walk around the perimeter of the grove which was in full bloom on this spring day. After they had walked silently, both in their own thoughts while enjoying the beauty around them and forgetting the previous violence they experienced.

"How good it is to be alive." Will observed.

"I was so afraid for you back there," Margaret said. "I've watched you fight it out with bad men and each time I prayed you'd come through unharmed. You did, but I admit that each time I seem to die a little inside, as do other wives of lawmen."

He turned and held her close to him. "I know, dear. The great secret is I do, too. But it's my job and someone has to do it and I am the man hired to do it. But I have faith the Lord will take me under his wing and keep me from harm, because my mission is an honorable and necessary one."

She smiled back, kissed him. "I know that and have adjusted myself to it, though at times it's a hard row to hoe, especially when we also have Tommy to consider."

"I know that too, Margie, but I solemnly promise I'll never put myself in harm's way deliberately."

"Then I promise to be behind you in everything you do, no matter where or what"

Margaret took in a deep breath, stared at Will for a beat. "One thing about you I admire is you never beat around the bush about things."

He smiled. "An admirable trait, don't you think?"

"At times, yes. But I want to make sure you're really comfortable in your job."

"I am. But we must get back. They'll think we're lost," Will said.

They turned and, holding hands, returned to the Grove where everything was going along greatly. All were having a good time as orchestrated by Arthur, Lucy and others.

Will and Margaret glanced at each other, smiled and broke into laughter, while Tommy looked at them, puzzled.

Arthur walked up to them. "Will, I heard from those present that those gunman planned to rob the bank. Is that right?"

"Yes, it is. They planned to kill me, my deputies and then rob the bank.

"Then I and the bank officers are grateful to you. I am aware you've not taken a vacation for a long time back. So I've spoken to the others and we've decided you need a vacation. We want to send you on one with all expenses paid."

"You needn't do that. I was only doing my job," Will said.

"I know that, but we're adamant. Reluctant or not, Marshal Will Howard, you and your family are going."

Back home, Tommy approached his parents. "Mother, Father, I don't think I should go with you on this vacation. You two have earned it far more than I. I'll stay with Uncle Arthur. Please don't argue me out of it. I insist on it and I'll be fine. You two have earned this vacation. I didn't."

Surprised, Will and Margaret glanced at each other. "Tommy, if that's what you insist on and want, it's fine with us."

To days later, Will, Margaret, Tommy, Arthur and a group of well-wishers stood on the platform of the railroad station waiting for the oncoming train chuffing in, tossing huge plumes of white smoke.

The bell-shaped stack of the locomotive emitted clouds of white smoke and the polished brass fixtures shone in the morning sunlight. Someone had placed a wreath of flowers around the stack's base, in a gesture of honor for the couple.

"Enjoy your vacation," Arthur told the beaming couple. "Remember, I've made reservations at the Mulebach, the best hotel in Kansas City."

"Thank you, father. That's most generous," a tearful Margaret said as she hugged and kissed him goodbye. Then she hugged Lucy and Jason before she and Will entered the first car on the 11:15.

With its whistled blowing shrilly, the train chuffed and clunked out of the depot, headed for Kansas City, Missouri, and the happy couple's honeymoon.

# CHAPTER 2

"So this is Kansas City," Will exclaimed as he and Margaret left Union Station the next day when riding in a buggy rented by Arthur for the newlyweds on their first day in that great city. "It makes Dodge look like a little village." Will observed.

"Yep," Dan, the buggy driver replied. "She's grown some real fast since the Hannibal Bridge was built in '69."

"Have you lived here long?" Margaret asked him.

"Yep, 'bout five years. Came here from 'Frisco.' It ain't as big as old 'San Fran,' but she's gettin' there. Keeps growin' day by day it seems. Gettin' to be a tourist attraction. By the way,

We're passing the fountains that made the city famous. Fact is it was used fer waterin'

hossses, But they's just landmarks now.'

He winked at them, "Things do change with time, don't they?"

"Amen to that," Will replied.

Dan clucked the horse to a halt before a large structure. "Well. here we are—the famous Muhlebach Hotel yer new home fer a spell. Built in 1816 and it's the best in these parts."

The couple stared at the huge building built with an ingenious combination of brick and wood,

Margaret felt a flush of excitement over their being in "KC" as it was always affectionately called by native Kansans. Her father had often related the most interesting stories about the fabled city, hen she was growing up.

"I suggest ye best eat dinner in the dining room, the finest in these entire parts. And don't leave without visitin' the Gayety Theater next door."

He glanced at Margaret. "It's billed as a burlekee house, but It has more vodvill and all that."

Margaret laughed. "Nothing can shock me, Dan. I'm not from the backwoods—I've already heard of burlesque"

"And I've not lived a sheltered life," said Will. "Even if I used to be a man of the cloth. So I too won't object."

Dan chuckled as he waved at a uniformed man at the entrance. "Howard there will take care of your luggage. Remember, I'm at your service, as long as you're here."

"Thanks, Dan," We appreciate it," Margaret said. "Come, Will, let's get settled in our new home here."

"It's fine with me," Will replied. "I admit I've always wanted to see more of Kansas City."

"Yer want is about to come true," Dan replied.

As a doorman took their luggage, the couple glanced over the huge entrance to the hotel and each marveled at the ingenuity of the men who planned and built it.

The lobby was large and ornate, in keeping with the reputation of the hotel. It was crowded with people from all walks of life late in this day, expect for tramp-types which were never allowed to set foot in it.

After registration with a balding clerk, Oliver, they were taken up an ornate stairway to the first floor and to their room which turned out to be as sumptuous as one would expect in a hotel of note.

"What elegance!" Will remarked as he walked around the room, examining this and that." Look at the draperies over the bed. Who sleeps here? A king or queen?"

"No," she remarked, coquettishly, "Just us and none else."

He came to her and swept her into his arms. "Yes, just us, my love."

He kissed her with all the passion he could muster. Then she went over, closed the huge drapes that made the room darker than outside. Taking her in his arms, he carried her to the bed and deposited her on it. He straightened the covers, plopped up the pillow and looked down at her.

"We've got business together," Will said, smiling broadly.

Before we get into a very private and intimate scene between man and wife, a curtain must come down on the scene.

The next morning, after a sumptuous breakfast in the hotel's very ornate dining room, Will and Margaret left on a tour of the city in the buggy that awaited them at the main entrance of the hotel, with Dan in the driver's seat.

"Before we leave, I want you to gaze at the next building to the hotel. That's the Gayety Theater, best durned burleqee joint in town."

Margaret looked puzzled. "Burlekee? What's that?"

Will laughed." I think he means 'burlesque.'"

She frowned. "Oh, that! Where women prance around almost naked? How disgusting."

"That may be so, Missy," Dan said, smiling. "But it's given us some great comedians and entertainers, like they have in London music halls across the old pond"

"Well, that's different," Margaret said, guardedly. "It sounds more intriguing."

Will laughed. "Now that is my girl."

She said, "As the inventor said, looked at looking at his first model of the wheel, "let's get rolling."

With everyone laughing, Dan whipped the buggy into motion and they were whisked down Wyandotte to Main Street where they were treated to the very heart of the city with it's myriads of shops and places of business.

As they went along, Dan commented," Old KC's grown to about 340,000 souls. One of the finest cities in the U.S. of A.""

When it was time for lunch, Dan took them to a small restaurant, Jacopo's, for lunch. He deposited them in front of the place.

"I'll be back in an hour or so," he said.. "If yor still not through, I'll park and wait for ye."

Alone on the sidewalk, Will and Margaret looked at the establishment.

"Doesn't look stylish," Will said.

"Maybe so." Margaret said, "But if Dan recommends it, it's all right with me."

As they turned to enter, a large rough-looking man was passing by and accidentally brushed against Margaret making her drop the parasol she was holding.

"Do ya want the whole sidewalk, Missy?" the man said.

Will confronted the man. "It seems you lost your manners, my friend. You bumped into her. Now apologize."

The man looked Will up and down. "You with her?"

"Yes," Will replied. "She's my wife. Now apologize, please."

"Ta hell I will. Wherdya pick her up? The burlekee? Looks like she'd make one hell of a stripper. Like to take her to my room for in good spell of rollin' in the hay."

That was too much for Will. "Damn your mouth!"

He grabbed the man by the coat collar, lifted him off the side walk and threw him down with a hard slam.

Badly shaken up by Will's strength, the man got to his feet, but being careful to keep his distance from him, he dusted himself off and started to move off. Then he stopped, turned and glared at Will who showed a clenched fist. "Want this?"

The man quickly moved off. as Will picked up the parasol and handed it back to Margaret, "That ruffian picked on the wrong person. Are you all right, dear?"

"I'm fine," she replied, straightening her dress. "It was nothing. Ruffians are everywhere, I guess. Let's go in. That didn't change my appetite."

They entered the establishment and found themselves in a small but stylish surroundings, with gas lights burning on the wall and flowing draperies around the door.

A man clad in a frock coat, Ascot tie and a flower in his lapel, approached them. "Welcome to Sargo's. I'm Gustaf, your maitre de at your service. Do you have reservations?"

"Yes, Mr. and Mrs. Will Howard,"

At the name, Gustav's face brightened. "From Dodge City?"

"Yes, we are."

He checked a book on the counter, nodded. "Ah, the famous Fighting Marshal Howard. We've been expecting you."

"Thank you," Will replied.'

"All arrangements for you have been made. Follow me, please."

He led them to an elegantly set table. A vase containing freshly-cut flowers graced the middle of the table and two uniformed men appeared and stood nearby, ready to be at their service.

"Looks like father didn't overlook anything," Margaret said, as they settled in at the table and accepted a large embossed menus. "I might have known."

"That's because he loves you, my dear. As you know, He'd move the world for you, if he were asked." Will replied. "Now let's eat."

"I guess so Look at this menu. Glad it isn't in some foreign language," Will said. "But I recognize a Chicago-cut petite steak when I see it."

Gustaf, hovering nearby, with an order pad in his hand, responded to Will's words: "A filet mignon for the gentleman. Excellent choice. And the madam?"

"I'll take the same. We Kansans cannot pass up good beef when we see it." Margaret smiled up at him.

Exuberantly, Gustaf took down the orders. "A bit of wine before, perhaps? Our house wines are the very best this side of the Mississippi."

As Margaret was rearranged items. She knocked one off the table.

Will to retrieve it,

"Permit me, please." This came from a nearby table. A diminutive Oriental gentleman had arisen from his table, retrieved the purse and handed it to her.

"Thank you, sir," she said to him,

The man bowed and smiled broadly. "It is my great pleasure, Madame"

He was clad in a tailored suit, white shirt and ascot tie. Will thought it to be quite different than other Oriental men he had seen. Will experienced a strange calm feeling in his presence.

He bowed again and returned to his table. Will also felt an admiration for the ease at which he moved which was almost cat-like.

"What a nice, polite man," she said to Will. "And he spoke good English."

"I noticed that, too," Margaret replied. "Perhaps he's some sort of diplomat."

"Whoever he is, he's a real gentleman," Will said. "Not many men would have reacted the way he did. They'd have a 'get it yourself' attitude."

"Very rare on this frontier," Margaret replied.

At this point two waiters approached the table, delicately balancing huge trays on their shoulders.

"Ah," said Will. "Our food arriveth and, not too soon."

The trays were heaping with food but all was overshadowed by the sizzling steaks, petite and juicy-looking with fried potatoes, big salads and all topped with a selection of fruit pies. Afterwards, with the tacit permission of Margaret, Will enjoyed a large, fragrant cigar.

"I didn't know life was so sweet," Will leaned back in his chair and blew smoke rings toward the large, ornate chandelier overhead. "Far, far better than anything in Dodge," he observed.

"Why doesn't Dodge have something like this."

"Someday, as it grows with the times, it will," Margaret replied. "Well, shall we depart? We still have much to see here in Kansas City,"

"I guess so," Will said, "Call Gustaf over and we'll take care of the bill."

When Gustaf arrived, he said, "All has been taken care of for you by Mr. Love. I trust you were satisfied with the food and service."

"Very satisfied,," Will replied," Thank you, Gustaf. Everything was superbly done, both the cooking and excellent service."

Exiting, they passed the Oriental man's table. He smiled and nodded at them. Margaret and Will smiled and nodded back.

"What a nice man," Margaret commented.

"Yes, I would like to know him better," Will replied.

Outside on the sidewalk, Will, noticing Dan in his carriage on the opposite side of the street. nodded at him. Then he and Margaret stepped into the street. They halted to allow a mule-driven streetcar to clop and rattle by, then they proceeded toward Dan and the carriage.

"Now let's see what more old KC has to offer." Will said, as they headed toward the awaiting carriage and an awaiting, smiling Dan. They noticed that he sported a newly cut flower in his lapel.

True to his professional calling, Dan took them on a whirlwind tour of the city, including a visit to the Delaware crossing where a ferry allowed settlers to cross the river.

And, of course, the fountains that made the city so unique were visited. As with most visitors to Kansas City before them, the couple was awed by the sights of that famous city.

At the waning of the day, Dan took the weary couple back to the hotel for a good meal and some rest. They enjoyed a scrumptious dinner of venison stew, boiled potatoes and a huge salad of local greens and fresh tomatoes.

"I hate to think of this wonderful time coming to an end," said Margaret in their suite, enjoying a late cup of coffee brout to them in an ornate polished container.

"All my life, in spite of a fairly good life my parents gave me, I have dreamed about something like this. It's my husband and I again enjoying our wedding feast."

"It's been a generous thing your father did for us. I could never have afforded it," Will said.

"I guess I'll always be his little girl," she replied. "Some- times I think he was spoiling me."

He put his arm around her. "Well, be that as it may, I'm glad he spoiled you. I want to spoil you even further.

He pulled her to him and kissed her long and passionately, before he got up, turned the gas lights off and returned to her in bed.

# CHAPTER 3

The trip eventually came to an end. The day of this dawned bright and sunny. The couple reluctantly packed their things and allowed Dan to also reluctantly take them back to the train depot for their trip back to Dodge City.

"If I be allowed to say so, I think you are the nicest and most polite and famous couple I ever had the pleasure to have in my carriage. And I darn well mean that." Dan said to them, as they awaited the train. He insisted he would stay until they were safely on board and on their way.

"Thank you, Dan," Margaret said, "You have been a good host to us and we won't forget you."

"And you were damn good guests," Dan replied, wiping a tear way from the corner of his eye.

To the amusement of observers, he gave each a big hug.

Dan waited until Will and Margaret were on the train, before he left the platform. "May the good Lord be with you two always,"

The couple's arrival in Dodge were met by a bevy of people, including Tommy, Arthur, Lucy, Willie Smothers and Mark Williams. To their surprise, Sam Oliver, retired sheriff, was there.

"Oh, I am so happy to se you both," said a tearful Lucy who almost did a dance of joy right there and then.

After hugging his parents, Tommy said, "Glad you're both home. I admit I really missed you. I helped Mark out at times."

"Appreciate it," Will said. "It seems you two did a good job. Things look peaceful."

"Oh, we arrested a couple of cowhands causing a ruckus at the Long Branch, but nothing; out of ordinary." Said Mark'

Satisfied over the apparent status quo, Will later plunged himself into his duties as marshal. Margaret, meanwhile, busied herself with the affairs of town, church and the arrangements for moving into a vacated house, near the center of town, bought with a bank loan backed by a note from Arthur.

Those duties took him back on his usual morning and evening rounds of the town. Checking supposedly locked doors of establishments and, of course, the Long Branch.

As he entered that establishment, he glanced around, visibly checking on everything. All seemed to be normal to him.

"Ya had an ace up yer goddam sleeve!" The voice came from a corner table, almost unnoticed by Will. He walked over to it. Three or four men were playing cards "Something wrong here?"

"Yea, Marshal. This yahoo's cheatin'" said a tall, lanky cowhand. Sonovabich has cards up his sleeve if ya ask me."

"Yer a damn liar!" said the other.

Suddenly, the tall man scattered the cards, upset the table and stood up, fists ready. "Come on, ya bastard! I'll Prove it."

Will strolled up ands faced him. The man was a few inched taller than he. "You won't prove anything, Mister. Now, clear out of here, before I throw all of you in jail."

His companion stood up, came to his side. "Stay auta this, Marshal. I just want a piece of this no-good cheatin' bastard."

Then Will became aware he wasn't wearing his pistol. The long, enjoyable wedding trip had caused his memory to slip a little.

One of the men noticed this fact. "Well, Marshal, ya ain't carryin' yer iron."

"Will shrugged his shoulders. So I did. Well, I won't need it. Come on, let's go."

"No we don't!" The taller man suddenly took a swing at him. Will ducked and the swing went wild. Will countered with a roundhouse punch. It sent the man crashing back into a table, scattering the contents and the men playing at it.

"Damn yer eyes!" The other man also took a swing at Will which he easily ducked. But, before he could do anything, he received Will's straight punch into his midriff that also sent him to the floor, writhing in pain.

Swiftly, Will walked over, scooped up the two ,and hauled them out of the saloon, by the scruffs of their necks.

Back in the Long Branch, one man at another table looked at his companions. "Looks like we got our fightin' marshal back."

The other agreed, as they watched Will carry the two battered thugs through the main door.

Will's reputation as continue to grow. Incidents of criminal activity began to decline and Dodge gained a well-earned reputation as a safe cow town. Men began to show up at his door, asking if there's a post of deputy marshal available.

Meanwhile, Will and Margaret continued their efforts to make their new home cozy and inviting to guests. Soon Margaret began to lose her energy drive and she felt lethargic more often than normal. Tommy always helped out as much as he could.

Will decided to call in the new doctor in Dodge, Phineas Novinson. The good doctor was a popular one in Dodge. His appearance always pleased new patients with his tall, well-muscled frame.

Moreover, the doctor's keen sense of humor always captivated his old as well as new patients.

"Well, mow, You look too healthy and sprite to be lethargic. Must be something else. Mrs. Howard. But let's take a look."

He opened his bag and rummaged around in it. "Now, where's my stethoscope. Can't do any doctoring without it, can I?"

He found it and held it up. "There's the conniving little bugger that no physician can be without.'

He enjoyed a laugh with the Howard's. Will was impressed with Doctor's technique of putting his patents with ease with his sense of humor.

Then the good doctor went to work earnestly and methodically. After a short examination, he rolled up his stethoscope, placed it back in his bag.

"Well, there's no need for alarm here, Mrs. Howard. To put it mildly, you're now again with child."

For a few beats, Will, Margaret and Tommy stared unbelievingly at the good doctor. He looked back at them, his eyebrows high.

"Why are you both all-fired surprised? You're married, aren't you? You have one child, why not another?

The couple then stared at each other, mouths opened. Then both broke into laughter.

"You're right," Will said. "It was wasn't unexpected soon.

as expected, Margaret fell into Will's arms, both laughing joyously. Tommy was pleased that he'll have a little brother or sister.

"Thanks, Doctor," Margaret said. "You certainly brought good news."

"I second it," said a jubilant Will.

"Then that's that," Timmy said. "And that's a fact."

They went into a round of hugs and kisses again.

Suddenly, Margaret was caught up short. "We've got a lot of things to get. Tommy's old crib for example. And we'll need--."

"---Whoa, there," Will said. "We'll plan that. There's that spare room. Nothing but junk in it. We'll renovate."

Margaret faced Will directly, put both hands on his shoulders. "Will, all this brings up one important aspect--your work, I want you to be especially careful from now on."

"Margie, never worry about me." He put out both fists. "I have these and they'll never fail me."

"And your gun--?"

He touched the Colt at his side. "And this won't fail, either."

"Well then, let's get busy," said Margaret. "We've got a larger family to plan for."

The following days were spent planning for the new addition to the family. Tommy was pleased over the prospect of having a brother or sister and promised to help take care of him or her.

The following months went by and all seems well and good in Dodge. The streets were free from disorderliness and crimes of any sort and it seems that Dodge was finally becoming an example of a tamed city on the frontier.

But that was soon to change.

Four men were meeting around a fire on the outskirts of Dodge. Three of tem were typical drifter types; the fourth was a hulking man sitting glumly aside from the others.

One of the men, a skinny disreputable-looking man, seemed to be in charge of the others.

"We got to get into that bank, somehow." He was saying, "They keep a lot of cash in there, put in by cattlemen to payoff their herd men." This from the obvious leader, Grat Wilson.

"Grat, yer forgettin' that marshal." Said one of the others, only known as Hank."He's a tough one, with those fists of his. He ain't called 'the fightin' marshal' for nothin.'"

"I agree," put in Cal Peters. "He's as good with them as he is with his gun."

Grat said, "Yea. I thought of that. I have them answer."

"And what's that?" said Cal Peters.

"Boris."

The men exchanged glances.

"Boris. Yea, why didn't I think of him?" Cal replied.

"But will he do it?" asked Hank. "He keep pretty much to hisself."

Grat produced a sly smile. "Don't you remember? His brother Mike?"

Recognition lit up the facers of the others.

"He was pretty rough on Mike," Grat said. "The marshal knocked him on his ass a couple of times and threw him in jail. Boris said he'd even things up. But he never did."

Grat's sly smile turned into a cruel one. "We'll have a talk and I'll tell him Boris is lookin' for him to give him a dose of what he gave Mike."

"Yea, that'll do it," Hank put in. "Boris's been waiting for a chance like that. He'll lay that marshal out."

"I know," said Grat. "I'll go see him."

Meanwhile, Willa, Margaret and Arthur were immersed in all of the ramifications of enlarging their house to accommodate a new member of the family.

"Nothing fancy, Will. We can't afford a lot of luxuries," Margaret said.

Will looked at her, a smile on his face. "Of course . But I do think it should be larger and attractive, without a hint of elegance."

He was to say something more, but she placed a finger over his mouth, and shook another finger at him..

"Hush, hush, Sire. I'm not decorating Queen Victoria's chambers, just our humble abode, my sire." Margaret presented a mock bow.

Will laughed, hugged her. "All right. Do what you must. While you're attending to the kingdom, I'll go on my rounds and attend to the business of Dodge City,"

"Fair enough," Margaret kissed him. "I know you will do what's right."

She left the room. Margaret and Arthur watched her go, then looked at each other.

"What a lucky man I am to get a wife like that," said Will "And how lucky you are to have a daughter like Margy."

Arthur beamed. "Don't you think I don't know that? Not only a great daughter, but a great son-n-law and with another child coming."

Meanwhile, after letting his thoughts coalesce, he decided that all's well and continued his walk down Front Street.

"Marshal!! Marshal! Come quickly. There's trouble in the ally."

A pasty-faced boy had approached him, his face red with excitment.

"Show me where," Will said. He followed the youth down the street and into an alley. There, facing him was Grat Wilson, Hank, Hal, Cal Peters and another man in the shadows.

"What's wrong here?" Will said. "You reprobates causing more trouble again?"..

"Naw," Grat said. "Just wanted you to meet someone that wants to meet you. Boris!"

As Will watched, a man stepped out of the shadows and stood before him. He was a huge one, taller than Will and with a big, powerful body to match.

"What do you want, Boris?" Will said, feeling a bit apprehensive.

"You," Boris's voice was deep and growl-like I tone. But it was his physique that bothered Will. He resembled a grizzly bear standing on his hind feet. Will felt it was a setup and he was to take this giant in combat.

Will looked at Boris. "Why are you doing this? What did I do to you?"

"My brother, Mike. Ya beat him up bad."

"Ah, yes, Your brother broke the law and resisted arrest. I had to do what any lawman would do in that case."

"He was beat-up bad," Grat put in. "More'n he deserved."

"He deserved it, all right," Will said, putting his hand near his gun rig. "Now go on your way or I'll arrest all of you."

Grath gave a cruel laugh. "Need that gun all the time, Marshal? What's wrong with your famous fists or is that a lot of bullshit?""

Will began to realize he had been backed into a corner on this. And must fight or lose his reputation as the fighting marshal.

There was not much Will could do. He was in a quandary. If he refused to fight, he'd be looked upon as a coward and lose his reputation. He decided to stand and fight despite the size and potential strength of his opponent. He removed his rig, laid it on the ground. "All right," he said. "Let's get this over with."

Inwardly, Will was by now really apprehensive, he wasn't sure he could take on this giant and win. But, damn it, he'd give it a real try. He turned, faced his adversary, fists ready.

Meanwhile, on the edge of the group no one noticed a slight man had slipped in to observe the proceedings.

Will said, "Well, you wanted it. What are you waiting for?"

Boris emitted a deep growl, clenched his huge fists and suddenly lunged forward, swinging. He momentarily lost his balance and swept by Will. As he passed, Will's clenched fist came down, with a strong blow between the shoulders. Boris staggered a bit, but quickly regained his posture.

"Come on, Boris," Will taunted.

Boris stood to his full height and, growling like an animal, lunged again at Will, attempting to get him in his huge arms. "I'll kill ya!!" he shouted.

"Well come on, try it," Will replied.

As Will circled, he passed near Grat.

Taking advantage of the situation, Grat thrust out his leg, temporarily tripping Will.

As Will staggered to regain his footing, Boris, moving swiftly for his bulk, lashed out with his huge fist, catching Will on the side of his head. He went down on his knees, dazed from the blow. Boris' companions cheered him on: "Move on him! Kill him!"

As Will staggered to regain his footing, Boris lashed out and caught him on the side of his head, this time below the temple. Will went down.

Dazed by the powerful blow, Will staggered to his feet, But Boris moved in and caught him in a bear hug in his powerful arms.

"Come on, Boris, squeeze the hell outa him!" Hank shouted..

"Yea, give him the death blow," echoed Cal.

Caught in a powerful grip, Will was helpless. Dazed and hurting, he waited for that final blow sure to come.

"Enough! Release him!" The Oriental man had stepped forward, arms stretched out. "You're killing him. It is not a fair fight."

"Stay out of this!" yelled Grat. . "Get lost, you little slant-eyed bastard, or I'll beat the hell outa you  too"

Grat attempted a swing at him, but the little man ducked it.

Then, swiftly moving around, fists close to his chest, moving with incredible speed, the Oriental caught Grat across the side of his neck, with a slashing blow from the edge of his hand.

Grat responded with a gurgling cry, as he went down sprawling on the ground.

Boris, seeing this, released Will who also slumped down. He stared incredulously at the little man.

"Who the hell are ya?"

The Oriental hen took a stance, feet apart, fists closed in circular motions. "You want fight. Come on." He said in an almost quiet voice. "Only fair this time."

Boris, growling again, lunged forward, huge arms reaching out. But the little man easily dodged and, as Boris went by, he bent forward, his right leg stretched out full length and with a wide swing caught Boris fully again on the side of his head. Boris went down on his knees. The little man circled around him his fist close to his chest..

Meanwhile, Cal stepped forward. "Why ya little bastard! I'll—"

Again, the little man's leg suddenly came up, took a wide swing, catching Cal squarely in the head, sending him backward and sprawling to the ground.

The other men stood, mesmerized by an action they had never observed before. "I never seen anything like it," one offered, his eyes wide.

Meanwhile, Boris struggled to his feet, partly dazed, but not out of the fight. The others stared incredulously at the little Oriental, mesmerized by this incredible display of fighting that was new to them.

Then Boris emitted an animal-like growl, "You--you--"

He again lunged forward at his opponent and again with a blinding speed, he Oriental suddenly seemed to lift in the air, twirled around and, as he came down, lashed out with his leg, catching Boris squarely in the face. The latter emitted a gurgling scream and with blood spraying from his nostrils, went down and sprawled out.

The Oriental turned toward Grat and Hank, legs apart, fists in a circling motion. "You gentlemen want more," he said softly.

"No, no, said Grat. He turned to the remaining others and said, "Let's get auta here." He and his partners got a semi-conscious Boris his feet and, half-carrying Cal, they staggered off.

The little man turned to help Will who was struggling to his feet.

"What happened?" Will said. He looked around, spotted the other men carrying off the almost-Boris. He stared incredulously at the little Oriental. "I don't know you, but whoever you are, I owe you many thanks."

"Kim Lee at our service. Your bruises will need attention."

"No, no, I'll be all right," Will replied. "I've had worse than that."

He stared at Kim. "I recognize you. You were at that restaurant in Kansas City. You were very polite to us.""

"Yes it was my pleasure to do so," he picked up Will's Stetson which had flown off in he fight, dusted it off and handed it to him.

"May I ask where you are from, Mr. Lee?"

"Korea. I am an attaché to your country. I was stopping over in Dodge City on my way to Kansas City."

"It was a lucky thing for me you were here," Will replied.

"I saw you and those evil men go into the alley," Kim said. "I instinctively knew something was   wrong, I thought I may be of help."

"Well,' said Will. "I'm grateful you did. But tell me, what kind of fighting did you use? I've never seen anything like it."

Kim smiled. "It is called Tang Soo Do, an ancient Korean fighting technique. I learned it when I was growing up in Korea. But I must add that you are very proficient with your fists....I believe you call it 'boxing.' In Tang Soo Do we also use our fists, but we use the leg as a primary weapon with its longer length. Now, are you sure you are all right? You have some bad bruises."

"Yes, thank you, I am." Will replied. "Doctor Novinson will patch me up. Will you teach me this Tang Soo Do---that is if you aren't too busy?"

Kim smiled broadly and made a smooth, precise bow.

"I will be most happy to do so. You already have required basic principles of fist fighting. It's just a matter of learning about the feet, with some judo which is basic Japanese wrestling."

"I would like that," Will replied.

"When I am through in Kansas City, I was to return to New York, I will stay here a few days and happily accommodate you. Now, if you are sure you need no more help, I must be on my way."

He bowed. Will returned the bow, turned and, with that cat-like smoothness, Kim Lee walked away and disappeared from sight. Will stared after him. "If that doesn't beat all. Tang Soo Do," He mused. "Can you believe it, Will. old boy? You most certainly have much more to learn. Boxing isn't enough."

Shaking his head in disbelief, he left the alley, Accepting some sympathetic remarks from bystanders who had witnessed the entire incident, but he staggered a bit to be kept from falling by Mark Williams.

"Wish I'd been there, Marshal. I'd stopped him from hurting you with the butt of my Colt."

"That's all right, Mark. I had all the help I needed."

"Yea, I heard," Mark replied. "Who was that little man that helped you? They tell me he could fight like a bag of wildcats."

"Yes, he could," Will said. Get Doc for me and when I'm patched up a bit, I'll tell you about that 'little man,' as you put it."

For days after. Rumors flew back and forth in Dodge about the incident. Many speculated about Kim Lee and who he was.

But no one could throw any light on the situation of the mysterious little figure, much less Will Howard, but he determined not to forget the incident and he felt he would again meet up with the mysterious little Korean.

# CHAPTER 4

In a few days, things began to settle down a little in Dodge. Will was patched up by Doc Novinson who lectured him on the art of keeping out of real harm's way, seconded only by Margaret who was deeply concerned about Will's welfare.

"Why did you go there alone?' he asked Will, as he was putting a plaster on one of Will's bruises.

"Simple, Doctor. I saw that the situation called for my attention and I went, confident that I could handle anything that may come up."

"Well it did come up and you paid for it," Novinson replied.

"I'll be fine," Will said as he put his shirt back on.

"If it wasn't for that mysterious little man, you might have been killed. Do you have a handle on him? After all, we don't know much about him."

"No, but I am grateful for him, whoever he is," Will said. "Besides, I have a feeling I'll see him again."

Will put on his shirt and left Novinson's office, headed for home where Margaret and Tommy were waiting for him. When he walked in, she fell into his arms.

"Thank God you're alright, Will."

"I heard about the fight," she said, tears flowing down her cheeks. "I was so worried about you I was going to come down, but Mark came here and assured me you were all right."

She examined his face. "Oh, you poor man. Do they hurt?"

"Not much, Margie. Doctor Novinson assures me I'll be all right. It'll take time to heal. If it weren't for Mr. Kim lee, it would have been much worse."

"You did well, Dad, No matter what others say," Tommy put in.

"I have never met a man like him," Will continued. "He could fight like a wildcat backed into a corner. He uses a fighting technique from Korea, It is called Tang Soo Do an Oriental marshal arts technique. He was fast with lethal-like leg kicks and punches, so swift it passed all comprehension. And, the good part is, Margie, He's going to teach me this technique."

"Why? You're a great fighter now."

"But nothing like that. If I had his capabilities, Will said, "I wouldn't have taken such a beating. But with him, I'll become the real fighting marshal."

She kissed him. "Whatever you decide to do, I'll be behind you all the way."

"And I will too, Dad." Tommy put in, "You'll really show them. I just know it."

"With you two rooting for me," Will replied. "I can't lose."

The next few days were filled with activities for Will and Margaret. A beaming, proud Albert Paulson, with Arthur Love in tow, took them through Wright & Rath's General Store, pointing out various products, and consulting catalogues for others, much to a growing hint of reticence by Will.

"Aren't we going overboard a bit on all this?" he asked Margaret and Arthur when they were left alone to peruse the catalogues. "Don't you think we should make such a display, considering I'm just a United States marshal with a commensurate salary?"

"My dear Will Howard," Arthur said. "Let not your heart be troubled. You must remember that I wish the best for my only family. Money is not an issue here. My only regret is that your angel mother isn't here to see it."

Arthur took him by the shoulders and looked into his eyes. "Will, you know I only want the best for my family.. We could sit here until doomsday debating this, but I only want All of us to be happy and expense is no longer the issue here."

"I know that," Will replied. "But promise you I will not allow things to become too extravagant."

"The only thing extravagant we want here, My dear is your love and devotion," Margaret replied.

That did it. It hit Will in both his heart and his pride. "All right, Margie. I'll go along with anything you want for our home. I guess I should be proud to show you off before the whole town to which, by the way, I should now be in attendance."

He leaned then kissed her and put his hand on Arthur's shoulder. "I guess we're both very lucky to have a family like this."

With that, he turned and exited the shop, leaving Margate and Arthur looking after him. Arthur shook his head and smiled broadly. "I say this with all my heart in it. We both have been blessed with Will in our lives."

"With all my heart, I second that." Margaret replied.

Back in the marshal's office, he went in and performed the usual duties of a lawman, checking the latest wanted posters, the mail and other duties of his office. He was also aware that Mark had gone out doing the rounds for him. He went through the wanted posters and halted at one. It was a poster warning about the William "Bill" Bright gang. The large amount of award money attested to the gang's great notoriety.

Will had no longer been seated when the door opened and an individual came in, with a flair and pompous-like attitude. Will stared at him with an interested and slightly amused attitude.

The stranger was clad in an expensive, but well-worn suit. A gold watch chain was draped across a slightly soiled vest over an ample belly. A black hat with a thick brim was firmly placed on a rather large head. He was carrying a cane with a delicately carved grip.

"Marshal Howard, I presume," said from under a flowing and slightly graying mustache.

"Yes," Will said, his interest captivated at the sight of this unusual-looking man. "What can I do for you? Pease be seated."

The man took out a handkerchief and dusted off the seat before plopping himself down with a flair of one very sure of himself.

'My good man the question is not what you can do for me, rather it is what I can do for you. He leaned on his cane as he spoke. his voice clear, concise and well under his control.

"Let me introduce myself. I am Cyrus J. McNamara, proprietor of the world-renown "Dr. Emerson's Traveling Exposition." We specialize in only the highest expectations of showmanship and medical expertise."

Will smiled at that. "In other words, you're a traveling medicine show with an obtuse name."

Cyrus stared at him for a beat, a puzzled expression on his face. Then he produced a gratifying smile. "Well, now, that is most surprising, a lawman with an education. I like that. "

Will smiled back. "Let's get around this exchange of wordage and get down to the reason you are here. You represent a traveling medicine show, a common factor on the frontier and you want to open it here in Dodge. Am I right?"

Cyrus stirred slightly in his chair, ostensibly and unexpectedly disarmed by this man's unexpected eloquence. Then he sat back and grasped the can's head more firmly. "I see you are a man well aware of the questionable ethics some showman supposedly have. Let me assure you. Our show has been well received everywhere we have played around the frontier and in a great many cases, we have actually been invited back."

Will sighed. "Let's get down to basics here, Mr. McNamara. Although I personally hold a jaundice  eye about the integrity of your show. As a lawman will not deny you the right to hold your show in Dodge. All I ask in return is that it will observe the most rigid standards of propriety and honesty. In other words, I'll not tolerate any charlatan activities or I'll come down on you like the business end of a carpenter's maul. Do you agree with these conditions?"

Cyrus became a bit flustered. "Well, Sir, I promise you an exposition of the utmost integrity for Dodge City. I am aware of your past reputation of a violent, lawless town. I can plainly see why this has happened with lawman such as yourself at the helm."

Will stopped smiling. "You may drop the flattering platitudes. I'm giving you permission to set up your exposition on the north edge of town in that vacant lot."

He reached in a drawer, retrieved a paper and shoved it across the desk with a pen and ink well. "Sign this and to show you I'm not an unreasonable lawman, I wish you well with the show and will drop in now and then to check if you're upholding your end of the bargain."

"Rest assured that I will do just that." Cyrus took the pen, dipped it and wrote his name with a flourish. "There, my good man. And to show you that I will adhere to your standards as stated, I invite you and members of your entourage to be my honored gests on opening day."

"Thank you, Mr. McNamara. That's kind of you." Will stood up, indicating the meeting was over.

Cyrus also stood up and, with his well-trained demeanor, bowed to Will. "I wish you a good offering to Dodge. Good day, Sir."

As he walked out the door and almost collided with Mark.

"Excuse me, Sir," McNamara said with a slight bow. With Mark staring after him, he entered and confronted Will. "Who in the Sam Hill was that? Looks live a showy kind of guy, if you ask me, Marshal."

Will laughed. "That may be a problem for a few days. I'll explain it later. Take over. I have to go and check up at home."

"How's Mrs. Howard doing?"

"Just fine. Keep an eye on things, Mark."

"Will do," Mark replied, seating himself in the vacated chair after Will left, Mark put his feet up on the desk and leaned back. "I wonder what that strange man wanted. Well, the marshal will tell me all about it."

Meanwhile, Will was walking along the wooden sidewalk alongside Front Street. He nodded recognition to various people as he moved along. Then he almost bumped into a diminutive individual. "Excuse me," he said.

"Hello, Marshal Howard."

Will turned and looked at the man. "Well, Mr. Lee, fancy bumping into you again."

Kim Lee smiled. "It is my pleasure. It was no accident, Marshal I planned it that way. I saw you coming and decided to re-introduce myself. I trust you won't take umbrage at my way of doing so."

Will sat for a few seconds, pondering the situation

"No I won't. But it's a good thing you did ," Will answered. "I was absorbed in the problems of my office and didn't see you."

Will thought Kim lee looked much the same as last time he'd seen him. He was still immaculately and stately dressed, as in keeping with the office of a foreign government attaché.

"I see you are doing well." Lee said. "

"As do I," Will replied. "I'm grateful we met and I've often thought about your fighting technique---"

"---Tang So Do."

"Yes, that's it. Will replied. "I've never seen anything like that before. I want you to tell me more about it."

Kim smiled. "I am not surprised to hear this. Occidentals know little or nothing about this fighting art. The technique goes back in Korean history for two thousand years. But telling you about it is one thing; learning it first hand is another. Let me give you some of the secrets of Tang Soo Do."

"I would like that, unless it'd be a bother to you. I only have a limited idea of how busy you must be," Will said, his interest at a great height.

"Fret not," Kim replied, smiling. "I will be most honored to teach you. I will be in Kansas City next week on my return to San Francisco. We'll do it then."

"That'll be important to me," Will replied, feeling a thrust of interest and hope. "I must add to the repertoire of my reputation as 'The fighting Marshal.'"

"My thoughts exactly," Kim replied with a wide smile.

Will reminded himself that he had rarely seen an Oriental smile before. But he concluded that the man's obvious training as a diplomat would consider proper appearances under all circumstances.

"I must be going. My train leaves in a half-hour," Good day to you, Marshal. I look forward to our next meeting."

"It's been my pleasure talking with you and I thank you for your offer." Will replied.

Lee smiled, bowed and again, with that cat-like swiftness, he was on his way and blended into the crowded sidewalk.

Will watched him go, his hopes growing with expectations. He was so absorbed thus that he failed to notice Margaret standing beside him, staring at the disappeared Kim Lee. Then he turned and almost collided with her. He swiftly gathered her in his arms and lifted her off the sidewalk. "Oh, Margaret, I just had the revelation of my life."

He let her down and watched amusedly as she straightened out her skirt from the encounter. "Who in the world was that.?" she said. "The oriental man again?"

"Yes," Will replied. "That was none other than Kim Lee, the attaché from Korea that got me out of that mess. He's going to teach me some techniques of Tang Soo Do."

"Techniques? Tang Soo Do?' she said. "Whoa, that's a mouthful. is that the Oriental fighting you told me about?"

"Yes. I'll learn some of those fantastic maneuvers. Isn't that great?"

She smiled, straightened out his color that was a bit ruffled. "It's that way of fighting using hands and feet, right? The man who beat all those bullies who attacked you?"

"Yes, he is. I'm sure that, using what he teaches me, I'll round out my self-defense capabilities. I tell you, Margie, I believe this will be one of the most important lessons I'll ever learn."

She came over, hugged him. "Then so do I. You always know what's right and will act accordingly. You've never failed to do that"

He put his hands on her shoulders and faced her squarely. "I don't know what I've done to deserve someone like you. But whoever or whatever it is I'm eternally grateful."

She laughed, kissed him: "As the flower said to the sun, 'I'm so glad you picked me to shine upon.' So you, dear Will Howard, are that sun in my life"

"With that ringing endorsement in my ears," he said, "I must make preparations for the encounter with 'Dr. Emerson's Traveling Exposition.'"

Laughing happily, Will Turned and headed back to his office, leaving Margaret standing on the sidewalk, oblivious at the curious glances from passers-by.

Dr. Emerson's Traveling Exposition soon opened on the vacant lot in record time and was proving to be quite an attraction to the citizens of Dodge and corresponding communities. The citizens of Dodge had never seen such an extravaganza before.

Two large wagons were placed in a semi-circle on the edges of the clearing and on the vacant area were three tents, each bearing signs, in the center of the clearing, the main tent was larger than the rest and it was the focal point of the exposition. Cyrus McNamara used it to pitch his goods that included bottles of Aphrodite's Miracle Elixir "to improve one's love life and general health." The other tents contained various acts that included "Jo-Jo the Dog-Boy " which Will suspected to actually be a young lad in a mask, and "Anna The "Bearded Lady." which also could be a fake one. But he decided not to interfere with the various acts and not to take the chance of destroying people's fantasies both old and young. The main goal is to keep the peace at the exposition and help guarantee a good time for everyone.

The first day of the exposition went by without any problems.

People flocked to the site, from around the area and surrounding communities. Will and Margaret joined them, watching the exhibits and the main tent show with amused interest.

In the "Anna" tent one man stood up and shouted his objections: "Ain't true! No goddamn lady looks like that?"

"Oh, yea," answered another. "You ain't seen my Cuzzin Myrt. She even chews 'bacca."

"So's yer old lady!" another shouted.

"Shut yor mouth or I'll punch yor teeth out!" the first man shouted back.

"Yea, you an' what army?"

Will stood up and addressed the crowd: "Let's calm things down here, folks. This is a show meant for fun and enjoyment. If you don't like it, leave. There are other attractions.  Any punching to do and I'll do it."

"We'll oblige, ya, Marshal," Said the second man.

"Good," answered Will. "That's what I like to hear. Remember the old saying: 'the show must go on."

The nervous cast resumed their parts and quiet became the rule under Will's threat of an iron fist control. During the vocal exchange, no one noticed that Jo-Jo the Dog-Faced Lady's beard had slipped a little.

The second day went without incident. Then things began to liven up as more and more trail drifters began to show up along with more dangerous-appearing men. He also began to suspect the "elixer" as having a little more alcohol than listed on the label. He decided to stay at the exhibit, with a couple of deputies, to keep an eye on things.

The second day went without any problems.

The third brought a minor incident, that foreshadowed what was to happen later. A group of Indians came to see the shows and there were some objections to their presence.

On man shouted, "Throw those injuns out! They don't belong here!"

"Oh, yes they do," said Will. "They have ad much right as you. Now shut up and get out or I'll throw you out."

The man stood, staring at Will for a time, but kept his peace.

"Then things came to a head when a big drifter stood up in the Anna tent and shouted, "I'd rather be seen with a dirty buffalo than these freaks!"

"Shut yor big mouth you big bum. Sit an' let us see the show,"

The drifter stood up to his full height and shook a fist at the man who yelled, "You're just full of Buffalo shit. Let's go outside and see if you're man enough to shut it for me.  Huh?

Huh?"

Will stood up and got between the two antagonists. He was a head shorter than the drifter, but he faced him squarely. For the first time he experienced an uncomfortable experience, not sure he could take the drifter. He decided to use tact instead: "Come now, mister, this is a family show with young people in the audience, you don't want to frighten them, do you?"

The drifter looked down on Will, his mind whirling with possible means of action. He was much larger and he was aware of his strength, yet he was being faced down by a legendary lawman.

"Well, do you?" Will said again, calmly.

The drifter shifted on his feet, obviously finding himself in a difficult position. He was aware of his own strength, but this man before him was the redoubtable Fighting Marshal.

"All right," he said, expelling his breath. "I'll apologize to the kiddies." He turned and exited the tent, along with a couple of his belligerent sycophants.

Then Will expelled his own breath, turned to the disturbed audience and said, "Folks go on with your fun. The danger's over."

A round of applause came from the audience. As Will was preparing to leave, a member of the troupe approached him. "Thank you for what you did. This troupe is grateful."

Will then exited the tent. Outside he was surrounded by Mark, two deputies and some male bystanders.

"Atta boy, Marshal, you faced that big critter down." Said one man.

"You're still our fightin' marshal," another exclaimed.

"Thank you, folks." Will said. "Now continue to enjoy the show. There'll be no more interruptions, I assure you."

After the ruckus had died down and the exposition went on as usual, Margaret dropped by and cornered Will: "Are you all right, Dear? Mark told me about that big drifter that challenged you. But you faced him down, like you have with others."

"Yes, Margie, but things were different this time."

"Different! How!"

"Last time I was sure I could outfight my opponents, but when I faced that big drifter, I felt doubt for the first time."

"Doubt? You? I don't believe it. You've never been afraid of anything. Will Howard. Not since I've known you."

They walked along, arm in arm, toward the office. "But I did. For the first time, since my last fight, I felt a bit of fear that I might not be able to take him. Imagine that, Margie, I, the so-called fighting marshal of Dodge City, feeling a modicum of fear."

"Fear is a natural instinct," Margaret replied. "Everyone feels it at one time or another. I have read that even some of the famous gunfighters have privately admitted feeling some fear when facing a dangerous man."

Will suddenly stopped, as did Margaret. "Margie, I really wish that Kim Lee will show up again."

She squeezed his arm. "He said he would and he will. Now let's get moving. We have some arranging to do in the living room."

Will shrugged. "Oh all right. If I must I must."

Margaret rolled her eyes and said, more to herself, "Men, they'll never change, no matter what."

Will's wish was granted, the very next day.

With the exposition over and forgotten, He was busy in his office, checking some bulletins that had arrived in the mail. Mark was at a desk nearby. The door opened.

"Good morning, Marshal."

Surprised, Will and Mark glanced up. Kim Lee stood there, smiling at him. "I assume all is well with you."

Will flashed a wide smile. "How nice of you to come."

"I know about your arrival this very morning and about your concern over my humble person."

Will looked puzzled. "You did? How could you? I'm puzzled, Mr. Lee. How do you do these things?"

Kim remained calm, a slight grin on his face.

"Never mind, Marshal, the fact remains I am here and that is most important."

"Enough said. By the way, thus is my deputy, Mark Williams."

With great interest on his face, Mark glanced up, nodded a greeting.

Will said, Now, Kim, what may I do for you.?"

"I am here to fulfill the agreement we had for you to learn fundamentals of Tang Soo Do. Are you available for this?"

"Yes, I am. When do we start?"

"At your convenience. Do you have a place where we can go?"

"Strange you should ask," Will replied. "There is an empty room in the building next door. I know the man who owns the space and I'm sure he'll allow us to use it. What is needed?"

"A large mat on the floor is sufficient for now"

"Correct. When do we start?"

"At your pleasure and convenience," Kim replied.

Will stood up from his chair. "No better time than now. Mark can take over the office."

"Sure thing, Marshal," said Mark, interest written all over his face. "I'll look over things. You can always count on me to help out." Then with a satisfied smile on his face, he left the office.

The room next door to Will's office proved adequate to Kim. "We'll need that mat for the floor," he said, scrounging around the room and its closets.

"Ah," he said. "this should do well."

He held up a large rolled-up rug . Kim said, "It has some thickness which could cushion the falls somewhat, although you may experience some hard falls I assume you'll absorb them, because you are well-muscled to begin with,"

"Very good," echoed Will. "Let's get started. Kim, you don't know how much I have looked forward to this. I can't wait to start."

Kim smiled. "A little more patience, my friend. Impatience breeds weakness. Your first lesson includes proper breathing techniques for conserving energy and building confidence."

"Don't we need uniforms of some sort?" Will said.

Kim smiled broadly. "Ah, you are aware we use some sort of uniform. It s called a dobok. I will get one or you from a friend in Kansas City who is able to get these things, including belts that show degrees in training, from white to black. But you needn't worry about that now. You are not going into combat at first. Perhaps later if you do well."

Will was pleased. He realized that this was something he had long waited for. Boxing gave him satisfaction in the realm of taking care of himself during any possible combat in any given situation.

In his work as a lawman, perfection as a fighter always seemed to be beyond his reach, that is, up to the point at which his recent experiences revealed.

"First, you must have proper breathing techniques to put your body in the proper spirit for training." Kim began. "Because of its importance, we will concentrate on that now and get to movements and strikes next time.

"Fine," Will answered.

"The purpose of your training will develop strength, speed, balance and flexibility which boxing techniques doesn't give you entirely

Now you must calm your mind and put all distracting thoughts out. Imagine a clear blue sky with floating clouds lazily drifting by. Your breath must come from the diaphragm and control of breath is important in this discipline. However, there is one thing I want you to implant firmly on your mind about Tang Soo Do and that is the goal of producing a mind at peace. Peace requires concentration and concentration means better balance. Balance obtains speed and greater power. It also requires controlled breath at all times."

Will nodded. "I will burn that firmly on my mind."

"That is so. I'm satisfied with your progress so far. Now let us proceed."

During the following, days, Will mastered the basics of the discipline. Later the rug was replaced by a mat which Kim had mysteriously found and the sessions became more comfortable to Will as he listened, practiced and gave even more practice. Kim also produced a dummy created from straw and cotton and hung from the ceiling for basic strike work.

Kim then energetically taught Will the basic strikes with the hands, fists and finally with the feet. Will was a natural, what with his long legs.

"I am please with your progress," he told Will, as they were resting with glasses of water that Kim encouraged him to get plenty of, in order to prevent hydration. They were thus engaged when Mark gingerly peeked in from the doorway

"Marshal, pleas excuse me, but your wife wants to see you right away. It's really important."

Will glanced at Kim. "Go," Kim replied. "It is something important, otherwise she wouldn't bother you. You have had enough for the day. We'll meet again tomorrow."

Anxiously, Will quickly dressed and headed for home, wondering what in the word could be so important she would interrupt his training sessions, outside of his regular duties.

He walked into the house and saw Margaret and Tommy.. "Sit down. We must talk, said she."

"Is it about my time with Kim Lee? I can explain that. I--."

"Hush, hush," she placed a finger on his lips. "Let me do the talking. I just came from Dr. Novinson's office and—"

He stood up, face taut with anxiety. "Something wrong with you?"

He bade her to sit down. Then he sat opposite her took her hands and looked into her eyes. "Nothing is wrong with me. Actually all is right. The baby is doing just fine. No worry about that. But guess what?"

Will was puzzled. He sat and stared at her, an incredulous look on his face. "Margiy, I don't like guessing games"

"No games." she replied. "Dr. Walker confirmed it I'm going to have a baby sister."

Then it hit Will. He jumped up and, to their amusement did a little dance. He encompassed them in his arms. "Wow! I'm going to have daughter. When is she due? How do you know it's a girl?'

"That's a medical secret, according to the good doctor It's too early to tell the arrival. We must go according to nature's time table."

"Well, another Son or daughter—it makes no difference, said Margaret. "The important thing is that we are having another child. We will love him or her, no matter what."

Will sat for a few moment, mentally digesting the news.

"How blessed am I for marrying you, Margaret Howard." he said, nudging her arm .

Suddenly, he remembered Kim Lee and the sessions on Tang Soo Do. "Damnit! how could I have forgotten Kim," he said. I must run and tell him the news. He plans to return to Korea "

He rushed over to the hotel and found Kim, sitting in the lobby, head buried in a small volume. He looked up, smiled benevolently. I was reading a copy of your 'Declaration of Independence,' by Mr. Thomas Jefferson whom I understand was a signer of one of the most important documents in the founding of your great country. Now I know why you Americans are so passionate about your heritage and you have done remarkable things in remarkable short times. It is a personal prediction that someday your country will be among the greatest of nations."

"We are well aware of that fact," said Will, pleased that Kim had not gone home. "Let me say how glad I am to see that you hadn't left for home. The good news is news was that we are having a baby girl."

"I assume he is sure of this?" Lee replied.

"Fact is, he is sure of it. How doctors know this so early is a mystery to me."

"Congratulations, my friend," Kim said. "A baby is a precious gift to a family. I am most happy for you and Mrs. Howard and Tommy. Now, Shall we cancel this session until a more appropriate time?"

"No. It is important I learn this," Will replied. "Your instructions shall go on as planned. Margie will understand."

"Then let's not waste any more valuable time." Kim said.

"How about right now?"

"That is fine, Will replied. "As the wise philosopher said, 'One must not waste time on frivolous things.'"

"Buddha?"

"No. Will Howard."

Laughing, They headed out the door.

The practice room had been considerably improved in the short time since Will had left. A few chairs were present with towels on them and a large mat graced the floor. The place was sotless.

Will was greatly pleased. "You've been busy here since I saw you last. Where in the world did it come from in such a short time?

"Never mind that, my friend. Now, for this, you must learn the earn proper techniques in the martial arts, as with any other endeavor."

"I agree with you," Will replied. "Now what do we do next?"

"First, we must learn the first and most important phase of your is a dunjigi against an attacker. Take a stance, please."

Will did so. Then he and Kim faced on the mat.

"I want you to throw a punch at me," said Kim. "And with all your strength behind it."

"Are you sure Kim? I throw a mean punch?"

"I know you do, but spare nothing,. Give me your best one."

Will balled his fists and, spreading his feet, prepared to throw a punch despite a slight reluctance against it. Then, with all his strength behind it, he threw the punch. With lightning-like speed, Kim stepped aside, grabbed Will's arm as it went by and the next thing Will knew he was flat on the mat, wondering what hit him.

"My God, what just happened?" He said, through a slight dizziness from the speed of it all.

Kim replied, "Always remember that balance, speed and power are vital to your technique." It is best practice against such attacks from fists such as you get here on the frontier."

He helped Will to his feet, bowed to him. "Remember to bow before and after each session. It is a sign of respect for your opponent."

"Be sure I won't forget it," Will replied, smiling.

After a short session, Kim announced: "I must depart now for unfinished business. But next I will show you the techniques of kicking blows, a basic part of Tang Soo Do."

"Be sure I'll be there," Will replied. "I thank you for the present instructions."

Kim grabbed his hand and pumped it vigorously. "No, it is I who must thank you for being an appreciative student."

As they prepared to leave, Kim said, "I have ordered a dubok, or uniform as you occidentals call it. It will be on the next train. If Mrs. Howard becomes ill, give her this. Very effective medicine."

He put a small package into Will's hand.

"Thank you. Now tell me how you learned all this?' Will said.

Kim said just smiled and nodded. "That should not concern you now, except that it is as it is. I will explain some other time. Now I must go. We will meet again at our chosen time."

He moved swiftly, deftly and disappeared, leaving behind a very contemplative and mystified Will Howard.

"Well, what must be must be," Will mused to himself. "I guess there are things I am not yet to learn. But for now I'd better attend to my duties.

To Will's satisfaction, the overall situation in Dodge was serene and without incidents. Of course the usual rowdy drunks had been arrested and tossed in jail, by Mark who was proving to be a real asset to Will. Fact is, Will was seriously considering making it known that, should anything happen to him, God forbid, Mark could efficiently take over the duties as marshal. It gave Will a peace of mind he needed during Margaret's late pregnancy and approaching birth of hers and Will's second child. He, Margaret and Tommy were in agreement that, beside that fact, Will should continue with Kim's lessons.

A three days they again met in the training room and, during the following days, Kim gave Will specific and rigorous training in the art of attack and defense of Tang Soo Do and some Judo.

"You learn fast and efficiently," Kim said after an unusually rigid and strenuous instructions in the spinning-hook kick which, according to Kim, is one of the most important attack moves in the repertoire of Tang Soo Do. During the first attempts, Will temporarily lost his equilibrium and fell flat on his face on the mat.

"At first if you--" said Kim, helping him up.

"--don't succeed, try, try again," Will interjected.

But Will tried again and again to finally succeeded, winning a round of applause from a very pleased Kim Lee.

"Now we will study defenses against group attacks. Then I must be on my way again. Always remember that balance makes speed and speed makes more power. You, my friend, have learned the secrets of one of the most efficient retinues of self-defense invented by man. It is far superior to the common fist-oriented boxing techniques of men on the frontier. You will have a great advantage over your opponent, with an ability they never dreamed of."

Kim paused for a beat, in order to deepen Will's attention. Then he continued: "To put it bluntly in your circles, 'they will never know what hit them.'"

"This has been the most important time of my life, Kim."

Kim faced Will squarely. "You must always remember to never abuse this knowledge. It was created as a defense mechanism and never, never as an aggressive one."

"Rest assured, my good friend, I will never forget that," Will replied, extending his hand. Kim took it and they shook hands vigorously. Their eyes met and something that was indefinable passed between them. A real and lasting friendship had been forged.

"I must leave now," Kim said. "I've neglected my duties long enough and my superiors in Kansas City want me to return."

"I understand." Will replied. "But you made one mistake."

Kim look at him, puzzled.

"You stated that they were your superiors. You're wrong their, my friend. "You're really their superior, whether or not they know it."

Kim said nothing, just bowed. "I will never forget you. We will meet again. I sincerely know we will definitely do so.'"

Then he turned and once again and swiftly left the room. Will stood, staring after him. "No, my friend, you are wrong. It is I who will never forget you, and we will definitely meet again."

Then Will put away some things and then, looking around the room for a spell, gave a big sigh, then exited.

After Kim left Dodge City, Will plunged himself into his job as marshal and that, coupled with Margaret's approaching birth date and Tommy's schooling, kept him busy for the following weeks. The town was growing larger in size and importance, as new people and businesses came in.

With that activity, Will's reputation grew as the "Fighting Marshal of Dodge City." Many people came to the town just to catch a glimpse of him and, if possible, meet him in person.

Then there were those unenlightened individuals who never seem to learn not to challenge the prevailing situation.

Will had just ridden in, did his rounds and was on his way back to the jail, when two men stepped out in front of him, blocking his way. Will instinctively moved his hand to his hip, to be near his gun, but suddenly realized he had forgotten to buckle it on when he started his rounds.

"Excuse me," he said. "You're blocking my way."

One of the two thug-likes and bigger of the two, glanced at his companion and said, "Well lookie here, now. If it ain't the big man hisself walking alone. Whaddya think, Bryce?"

The one called Bryce, snickered though his unkempt beard, "Well snicker me if it is. Don't look so good now without his gun, does he, Lou?"

"Not like the fightin' marshal he's supposed to be," Lou said.

Here we go again, thought Will. Many people never learn anything from history. Oh, well, it goes with the territory. Now his marshal arts training will come into play. In a way, he should have realized it would be so before long.

But one good thing about it all, he concluded, is they have no idea of his capabilities now, without a gun and just his fists.

"I'm figgeerin' those fists of your'n won't be much good against the two of us." Said Lou. "Bryce here is boxing champ of Wichita last year."

Bryce balled up his fists and assumed a fighting stance. By now a sizeable, curious crowd sensing blood had gathered.

"Well," said Will. "It's a shame you don't consider other people's capabilities, Lou."

Bryce glanced at Lou, "What's he talkin' about?"

"Damned if I know," Lou replied, "C'mon, Marshal, put 'em up."

Will shifted his stance slightly, almost unknowingly, with his right foot slightly behind his left. "Oh, well, don't say I didn't warn you,"

"Ha," Bryce replied, "No warnin.' Just fightim!'.

"You mean like this?' said Will, as he suddenly crouched and, with lightning speed, he leaped into the air, his right leg pulled close to his chest. It lashed out strait forward and plunged into Lou's sternum, sending him flying back and flat on the floor.

"What the hell!" shouted Bryce, staring down at his prostrate partner. Then he looked at Will who had assumed a fighting stance.

"You like hell, Bryce?' Will replied. "Maybe you'd like to go there."

"You bastard!" Bryce threw a punch at Will's face.

Will deftly stepped back and, as Bryce's arm went past his head, he grasped the forearm, straightened it and lifted it over his head. Then, pivoting on his right foot, pulled the arm down, like a lever, sending the big man over his back to crash on the ground where he lay spread-eagled, gasping for breath, the fight having gone out of him.

"Had enough?" Will said, still assuming his fighting stance.

Bryce moaned, tried to get up, but felled back. He and his partner were beaten men.

The crowd moved in, fascinated by what they saw.

"Ain't seen anything like it," said one man.

"Threw him around, like a rag doll," said another.

"Used his feet, too," said still another. "Fast as hell, it was. Never in my born days, did I see anybody fight without fists."

Then Mark came running up. He glanced around at the two men on the ground, then at Will. He sighed. "I might have known it would happen like this."

With Mark helping him, Will managed to get the two dazed and bleeding men to their feet.

One man came up. "Marshal, we know you're damn good with yer fists, but you didn't throw one punch I could see. What was that fightin' you used?"

"It is called Tang Soo Do. A Korean marshal arts," Will replied.

"Damned if I know what he said," remarked a bystander. "But whatever it was, it did the right job."

One man said to the others, "That explains what he was doing in the empty lot behind Arnie's shop fer a long time with that little Chinee guy."

"Yes," said Will. "I was well-trained there. That 'Chinee' guy was my friend Kim Lee a martial arts expert from Korea."

Two men looked at each other. "Don't know what is," one offered, "but it was a himdinger. He took down that big guy and another tough one. In one fell swoop he did."

He looked at Will, with growing admiration on his face. "Whatever it is and whatever you can do, you are for 'eartain our fightin' marshal and that's a fact."

Smiling broadly Will thanked him and then, taking Bryce's arm and together with Mark they led the beaten prisoners off to jail which was watched by awe-struck spectators.

# CHAPTER 5

Will's reputation as the Fighting Marshal grew even more after the marshal arts fight. Dodge citizens were filled with wonderment over their lawman who seemed to be full of surprises. His new fighting technique that didn't depend on fists and guns puzzled the residents and surrounding communities. Will Howard's reputation was now secure in the minds of all who knew him and those who heard of him.

But Will, who failed to bask in the warmth of his newly won reputation, moved about with the usual self-absorbance and dedication to his job. Even his deputy, Mark Williams, seemed to be in perpetual awe over his boss's newly won reputation.

"Marshal," he asked, "do you think you can teach me this Ta-ta...?"

"--Tang Soo Do," Will replied. "I thought about that, Mark. And I decided to teach you the fundamentals of the technique. The name means 'Way of the Chinese Hand.' It goes back to the Tang Dynasty from 612-907 when the peasants had to defend themselves against the soldiers of the ruling class."

"Well, whatever it is gets the job done every time," Mark answered, shaking his head as if to put finality to his statement

Will was gong to reply, when a man burst into the room. "Marshal, yer'd better come. It's important."

Will sighed. "Another drunk whooping it up at the Long Branch?"

'No, sir. About your wife."

Will jumped up at that. "Is she all right?"

"I don't know. I wuz just told to come get yer. Yer wanted at home."

Will sprung into action. He grabbed his hat and jammed it on. "Take me to her."

When they arrived at the house, the good doctor was at her bedside. Margaret. Tommy and Lucy McMillan were in attendance. He went to Novinson: "Doc, is she all right? Something wrong?" His face was taut with apprehension.

"I really don't have a handle on this yet, Will." Novinson said. "She has a high fever and some spots on the inside of her mouth, similar to those of measles. But that malady is usually for children, not adults."

Will went to her bedside. Margaret's face was white from exertion. She reached out to him and he took her hand. She managed a slight smile through the pain. "Thanks for being here. What about the baby?"."

"Hush, dear," Will replied. "You're in the capable hands of Doctor Novinson. He'll see you through this. I promise."

Margaret tried to answer, but fell back, unconscious.

"Doc?" Will looked at Novinson.

"She slipped into a mild coma," The doctor replied. "All we can do now is watch her, give her some mediations. I'll research this. I don't yet know about the baby, but the next days are crucial."

"Thank you, Doctor, I know you'll do the best you can."

"Dad, will Mother be alright?" Tommy's face reflected his deep concern.

"I don't know, son, but I have faith in Doctor Novinson and, of course, the Lord. We we'll pray hard for her recovery."

"I'll sit up with her tonight," Tommy offered. "It's the best I can do."

"Thanks, son," Will's voice was tight fro his deep concern. "I know the Lord will watch over her and send her the right treatments."

Night came and Margaret's condition began to deteriorate. Margaret and Tommy shared their deep concern, each taking turns sitting up with her and each praying to the best of their abilities. As time slipped by it began to look hopeless for Margaret. The baby came and was still-born. That brought heavy sorrow to Margaret, Tommy and Will. Mourning was postponed for later.

Then Kim Lee appeared.

Margaret and Will were sitting with her when Kim came in, almost silently. One moment he wasn't there, the next he was standing in front of them.

"Kim!" Will almost shouted his name when his friend appeared;

"I came when I first heard of her illness."

"But how did you--?"

"—know? We won't discuss that now. Come. Let me see her"

As they watched, Kim went to the bed, his eyes scanning the inert, pale figure on the bed. First hee examined her eyes carefully and ten turned to Will. "She obviously has lost the baby. Do you still have that packet I gave you?".

"Why, yes I do. It's in the dresser drawer. I'll fetch it."

Will quickly and methodically fumbled in the drawer until he found the packet wrapped in brown paper. He handed it to Will.

"Get me a glass of water and a teacup."." Kim said.

When he received the water, He carefully unwrapped the paper, exposing dried leaves. With the spoon reversed, he he carefully mashed some of the dried leaves into a fine powder. Then he went to Margaret. Sitting at her bedside, he slowly and carefully lifted her head a bit. He put some of the powder in the spoon, added a bit of water from the cup and mashed it into a paste. With the others watching as if mesmerized, Kim slipped some of the paste into her moth and carefully stroked her throat to ease the paste down. He followed it with another spoon of water.

"Now she must wait," Kim said, gently lowering her head back on the pillow. "I will sit with her for a spell, before giving her more of the potion. Meanwhile you get some rest."

"What will you do?" Will said.

"I will sit with her and administer the potion as needed until she begins to respond. Meanwhile you rest. You will need your energy when she begins to recuperate."

"I will do just that, Kim. I have implicit faith in you and I know Margaret's in good hands, my friend. Please don't hesitate to awaken me if I can help or if there's a positive change."

"That I will do," Kim responded. "Get some rest now."

Will retired to his office and literally dropped on a cot he had placed in a corner. He sat, bowed his head.

"Please, Lord, My prayer is that Margie will recuperate from this. I know that I am not a servant of yours as I once was. but I still love you, trust you and try to serve you the best I can in my duties. Also give comfort to Tommy, Arthur and all he others concerned about her."

Then he lowered himself onto the cot and fell into a deep sleep.

"Wake up, wake up, my friend," The voice was that of Kim's and it penetrated the deep fog Will was in from his sleep. "You've had the sleep of the dead and that is good."

Will rubbed his eyes to dissipate the fogginess. "Margie? How is she? How long have I been out?"

"One question at a time, my friend," Kim said. "You've been asleep for many hours. She is beginning to respond. It will take some time yet, but she is out of danger."

Will literally leaped out of bed. "Better? out of danger? What happened?"

"Come and see for yourself," Kim said.

Together they went into the bedroom where Tommy and Doctor Novinson awaited. Margaret was sitting up, slightly elevated.

Will went to her, gook her hand. She managed a weak smile. "Hello, dear. What took you so long?"

Will was flabbergasted. He could barely believe what he was seeing.

"She has responded to treatment and is on the road to recovery. I'm afraid we lost the baby," Kim said. "But your wife is fine."

"I must say," Novinson put in. "I was first very skeptical when I was told about you and the potion. As a doctor I was supposed to be skeptical, but I'm a practical man as well and I must admit the ancients knew more than we know. I'm amazed at what I've seen."

Kim smiled. "You are correct in your analysis. My ancestors had knowledge of this for many centuries. I humbly brought this knowledge into being. I take no credit for its success."

He turned to face Will and Margaret. "I must depart now for, how long I don't know. Just keep giving her the potion until she's completely cured which shouldn't take much more time."

"Will we see you again?" Will asked.

"I don't know, my friend. It depends on circumstances. But never fear. I'll be nearer to you than you imagine."

Will moved to grab his hand, but Kim deftly turned and left as mysteriously as he appeared.

"Damn it," Will said. "I just wanted to show my appreciation>"

"I think he already knew that," Margaret said.

That night Margaret lay asleep in Will's arms while he quietly stroked her head. He thought about her narrow escape and the coming trauma over her baby's loss.

The calm was broken the next day when Mark came into the office. "Marshal, there's trouble at Alice's. We'd better get over there pronto.

Will grabbed his hat, nodded at a lady who had been hired to care for Margaret. With Mark at his side, he walked up Front Street a bit then stopped and walked parallel to the Sante Fe tracks that bisected the town. He headed up West Street to a fairly well-kept two-storey house. Because of the notorious nature of that section, Mark carried a Winchester rifle, along with his gun rig. The street was almost vacant, telling Will that something big was brewing.

"I don't like this part of town," Mark said.

"I know," answered Will. "But even prostitutes must live in peace, like common folk."

"I don't know about that," Mark said, snuggling the rifle under his arm. "Far as I'm concerned, run them outa town."

"Just think, Mark, what it would be like on the frontier without the natural needs of drovers and cowhands weren't taken care of. Those 'soiled doves' are sorely needed."

Will knocked on the door of the house. In a moment, it was opened by a seedy-looking man in a derby hat and a cigar in his mouth.

"Glad you're here, Marshal. All hell's broke loose up there. Sweet Alice is fit to be tied, she is,"

'Thanks, Professor," Will said. "We'll look into this. Is she in the parlor?"

"She's got a rifle and she's fixin' to use it." Hester replied.

"Come, Mark. This may not be pleasant."

As they walked upstairs, Mark asked: "is he really a professor?"

"No. It's a name, commonly used in sporting houses and brothels,  for the piano player."

"He looks like no professor, to me," Mark commented.

As they walked through the parlor, Mark took notice of the fancy draperies, sofa, fireplace and carpeting. A brand new piano stood in one corner. He had a fleeting thought that all this was wasted on whorehouses and the so-called "soiled doves" that worked in them.

When they reached the first floor, a big black man with a large scar on the left side of his face stood in their way. "You can't go in there. Miss Alice said so."

"Come now, Alvin, you know it's part of my job. Now move aside, please."

Alvin put his big hand on Will's chest. "Sorry, Marshal, no."

Suddenly, Will clamped his hand over Alvin's and twisted it back. Alvin's face  became distorted with pain. His mouth popped open and he fell to his knees obviously in great agony.

"Now, Alvin, we're going in there and you won't interfere, understand?" He seemed to put pressure on the hand and Alvin uttered a cry of pain then a choking "Y-y-yes-s-s, Sir."

Mark watched this maneuver with intense surprise and interest.

Then Will twisted the arm to the side and, using it as a lever, thrust Alvin's big body aside and on his knees where he kneeled writhing in pain and holding his wrist.

"My God, how did you do that?" Mark asked.

"I'll explain later, let's go in."

Will opened the door and he and Mark stepped into the room. They were both stopped by the sight they saw. A frightened man stood on the bed as a rather large woman, dressed in a white gown with a slit side and a deep décolletage. stood on the left side. Her brown hair was smartly coiffured. A faint hint of rouge tinged her cheeks.

She gave Will and Mark only a slight glance. "This is personal business, Marshal. Nothing for the law to be concerned about."

"Oh, yes, it is, Alice. Anything that threatens a citizen is a concern of mine. "Now, put aside that scatter gun and let's talk."

"Sorry, Marshal, but this is betwixt him and me. I'm sick of bloodsuckers like him, trying to muscle in on my business. A lot of ladies think so and we're willin' to fight to stop it."

Her use of the word "ladies" caused Mark to snicker, but Will silenced him with a "no nonsense" look.

"Look, Marshal," Alice said, holding the shotgun steady on the cringing man. "We girls have a good business here on the frontier and you know it. Without us, a lot of daughters and sisters would be raped by some men in these parts and you know it. We do a service for the community and you know that.

"Yes, I do, Alice," Will said, keeping his eye on the shotgun. "But killing them isn't the answer and, I might add, you're aware of it. Now put down that scattergun and let's talk this over. I don't want to arrest you for killing this man.

At this, Alice softened. She lowered shotgun cradled it in her arm, muzzle pointed at the floor.

"Look, Marshal. Whether the good citizens of these parts know it or not, this is a needed business and we try to run it as one. We don't want any blood-sucking, so-called 'organizers' muscling' in on our business. Now throw him out of here or I'll blow that worthless part of his body off."

The man on the bed squealed in fear. Then he said, "The bitch is crazy, Marshal. I'm only doing my job."

"What's your name?" Will said.

"Grant Williams of the local chapter of—"

"Never mind that," Will cut in. "Let your organizers fight over this. I don't want it on my watch. Now get out, or I'll arrest you for pandering."

Grant scrambled to leave the room. He opened the door then turned to face Will. "This isn't the last of it, Marshal. You'll be hearing from me again."

"I hope not, Williams," Will answered. "For your sake that is."

Will moved toward him, but Williams quickly turned and ran out.

"Thanks, Marshal, Alice said. "Scum like him are leeches. Always trying to shake down people for a phony promise of protection. Much obliged or your help."

"That's all right, Alice," Will replied. "But try to keep order in here, will you? I don't want to keep coming to straighten out your problems."

She nodded her approval. "Will do, Marshal."

Will stepped into the hall, but halted to look at Alvin was kneeling on the floor holding his arm, his face still reflecting pain.

"I Alice should get another bouncer, Alvin here's not so good at his job."

Will and Mark left the sporting house and headed back up front Street.

"Marshal," Mark asked as they walked along. "I often wondered why so many women become spoiled doves."

"There are many reasons, Mark," Will replied. "The most common are running away from home, because of rigid and dominating parents. It's the only way they can make a living. Others are abandoned girls for some reason or another, Then there's poverty that drives them away and there's always illiteracy that forces young girls to advance themselves. There may be other reasons, but those are the main ones."

"Wow," said Mark. "Guess I led a sheltered life."

Mark laughed. "Oh, I don't know about that. You know a few things about life for your age and that's what counts, as far as I am concerned."

"Thanks, Marshal, I appreciate it. Can I ask another question?"

"Sure."

"I was wonderin' if you could teach me that...you know...that Ta-ta--"

He emphasized his words with a kick in the air.

"Tang Soo Do."

"Yea, that's it. Will you?"

"Yes, Mark. I think it's a good idea for lawmen to learn another type of self-defense, besides fists and guns."

They walked a bit, then Will suddenly stopped and faced Mark.

"You gave me an idea, Mark. Maybe someday I'll organize a school to teach Tang Soo Do. There are other forms of marshal arts; judo, karate, king fu just to mention some."

"Great," said Mark. "I'd consider it an honor to be one of the first students."

"Then so be it," said Will, smiling broadly.

Meanwhile at home, Margaret was slowly reconciling herself with the loss of her baby. After crying for a time, she came to the conclusion that life must go on and other babies can be had.

Will went through a short time of sorrow with her.

"On the frontier men have to steel ourselves against things like that," he said . "When the time is ripe we'll have another child."

Margaret slowly came to realize he was right and she set herself on the road to recovery, emotionally as well as physically.

Back at the office, things were quiet again. All seemed to be normal in Dodge City.

At least for the time being.

# CHAPTER 5

In a seedy Topeka building  two men were holding  a conference, in a smoke-filled room, at a table covered with cast-away cards, bottles and glasses. One man seemed to dominate the group.

He was heavyset with large prominent sideburns and an equally large mustache. His entire demeanor was one of a man of means, a "dandy." He held a cigarillo in his right hand that sported a large opal ring.

The other was a short, devious-looking man,  Barth, with weasel-like eyes and unruly hair black hair.

"Are you sure this man can take on the Marshal?" asked the heavy-set one.

"Yea," replied Barth. "He was three times champion boxer of Kansas City. No one could beat him. Goes by the name of "Groat." He's a mean one, he is."

"Sounds impressive," the Dandy responded.

I ll say. In his last fight he knocked out Willy Wilson right after the bell sounded. He's fast wit his dukes and knows how to use 'em. Why, one time he punched a hole through a door, when he he got pissed at his whore."

The Dandy sat, saying nothing, for a beat. Then he replied: "If he's so good why's he willing to help you?"

"Well, replied Garth. "And he ain't had a fight in a long time now and fights are hard to come by these days. Remember, no one's supposed to know this."

"On my sainted mother's grave, You have my word. I'll say nothing' to no one." The Dandy answered.

Garth then eyed him over from his fancy derby to his expensive, velour vest and Ascot tie. "If it ain't any of my business, why you want this fight with Howard?"

The Dandy looked grim for a beat, then replied: "You're right. It isn't any of your business, but I'll tell you anyway. This lawman parades around flaunting his reputation as "the Fighting Marshal." Because of him my business has suffered."

"You mean the whores of Dodge?"

"These girls are legitimate The very best in Kansas. There's none better anywhere."

Garth snickered at this, but the Dandy stared hard at him for a beat. Then he continued, "They are not crib girls or so-called' soiled doves'. They're from good stock and are pretty as a picture. "You mean they're high-class and men pay to spend a night with them.' But what's the marshal got to do wit' this?"

The Dandy looked incredulously at him.. "Don't you get it, you idiot? They're for hire, not something off a table. The Marshal thinks it's illegitimate business and wants it stopped."

"How's beatin' him in a fight goin' to do that?"

The Dandy gave him a look of disgust. "Look here. If his reputation is questioned, his influence goes down. Don't you see? If folks don't respect him anymore, we can't go on with our plans about organizing the pimps around here."

"Yea, If you kin do it," Replied Garth.

"I can and I will. You can take it to the bank,"

Garth studied him a moment. before replying. "Now get hold of your contact with this fighter and tell him we'll reward him well." the Dandy added.

Garth ran a hand through his unruly hair. "Okay, I'll do it. You'd better pay him or he'll rough us up good."

"My word is my bond. So get busy."

A few days later, Will Howard returned to his office, after a morning of rounds. He was content because all seemed well.

Even though it was nightfall, he started looking through wanted posters and the some papers that had piled up on him. Suddenly the door opened and Mark came in, all out of breath.

"Marshal, come quickly. It's your son Tom"

"Is she he right?' Will responded. "Did something happen to him?"

"Don't know. A man cane to me with the message from your Mrs."

Will grabbed his hat, jammed it on and headed for the door, followed by Mark.

At home, he was met by Arthur.

"What's wrong with him? Will asked. "Has he been hurt?"

"Yes. He's been roughed up by some young hoodlums," Arthur said. "He's not hurt badly, except for his pride. He's in his room with his mother and Lucy.

They entered Tommy's room to find him in bed being tended to by the two women. His face was bloodied up a bit and his right eye was ringed with black.

"They roughed him up," Arthur said to Will. "But I think he'll survive. He's pretty tough."

"Can't you do something about it?" Margaret said. "The streets aren't safe with those hoodlums running around."

"They terrorized some women a week ago," Lucy added.

Will winded at this. "Who were they, son," will asked. "Have you seen or recognized any of these men before?"

"It was dark and didn't see any of them plain." Tommy replied, wincing a bit. It was obvious he was reflecting some of the pain he was suffering. "But I think it was that gang led by Jim Pickler. He's a big bully"

"Exactly what happened? Where were you?"

"They bushwhacked me, as I passed an alley next to Front Street. There were four of them. I think I hit one or two, but there were too many."

Will closely examined the wounds on Tommy's face. "They did a job on you, but nothing that won't heal in time."

"I bet if I could fight like Mr. Lee, I'd fixed them."

"That's true. I tell you what. I'll teach you some defensive moves How's that?"

Tommy grinned widely. "That's be great, Dad." But now I'm tired and Doctor Novinson's on his way to patch me up."

"Fine. Meanwhile, I'll have a word with the parents of those hoodlums. You get some rest. Margie, I want a word with you outside."

In the hall outside Tommy's door, Will confronted Margaret, "Now I know what you're going to say. You don't want him to learn how to defend himself from Bully's."

"Yes, I was," Margaret replied. "Only you're wrong there on one count. I agree he needs to learn how to defend himself, like his father, but he must pledge not to bully others with that capability he learns."

Will looked at her, with surprise. "How I wanted to hear that from you. I thought you'd object to his learning how to defend himself. Tang Doo Do will teach him that."

Margaret smiled, kissed him on the cheek. "You underestimate me, Mr. Howard. I know what it's done for you and I want my son to protect himself in this lawless society, as his father does. I want him to be like you. So teach him well."

"I consider it a compliment," Will said. "I'll start tomorrow, because won't hurt so much to move around anymore. I must say, my dear wife, you delightfully amaze me with your insight."

"I had a good teacher," she said, kissing him again..

The next day they assembled in the old house that served as Will's practice room. Will was wearing his dubok, and Tommy was clad in a long underwear bottom. Will laughed. "You look like John L. Sullivan"

"Who's he?"

"A great boxer. You don't know of him, so never mind that. Now pay attention to what I am going to teach you. Tang So Do is an ancient fighting technique used many centuries ago.

"They were up against soldier's spears and shields, right?"

"That's right," Will replied. "All they had were their feet, and hands which they trained to be weapons, the only ones they had."

"Watching you and Mr. Lee, I have to say they were pretty good weapons.'

Will looked at him in amazement. "You watched some of our training sessions?"

"Yes, Dad. Couldn't help but doing so. You were practically in our back yard, you know."

Will laughed. "Well. I guess there wasn't anything secret about it. Now, for a beginning. Come at me and try to hit me with your fists."

Tommy's face was filled with surprise "Really? I might hurt you."

"Oh yea!" Will moved with lightning speed, stepping in and before Tommy could gasp in surprise, he was on the ground, with his father holding his hands by the wrists behind him.

"Ow!, ow!" Tommy was clearly in pain. But Will just as quickly brought him back on his feet.

"How'd you do that?" Tommy gasped, holding his wrist.

"Speed, surprise and power. You'll learn that in due time with a lot of practice."

Tommy again tried to hit his father and again he was rebuked and immobilized.

When he was back on feet, Tommy asked: "Will you also teach me that leap-up-and-spin-kick you use?"

"Of course. But in due time. It's the spinning crescent kick and it's complicated," But first earn the basics. It'll take time. I'll allow doing that on that my schedule then I'll teach you some very basic kicking techniques. Ready?'

"Ready when you are. Lay on, Macduff," Tommy answered.

Will laughed. "Touché! I have a feeling you'll make a good Tang Soo Do fighter yet."

Will and Tommy met at the lot for the next few days. He was a good student and learned basic techniques quickly, to Will's satisfaction.

A few days later, Will was in his office, when Garth entered. He was still impeccably dressed and carrying a false but disarming smile.

'Is your man ready, Marshal?"

Will stared hard at him. "Ready? What are you talking about?

"Your man is to meet mine in combat to determine which is the greater fighting technique. We want to prove that the old-fashioned fisticuff way is the best still."

"Oh, yes. but I didn't agree to this officially, you know, Garth."

Garth flashed a cold smile. "In fact you did, Marshal. No doubt you forgot it. That's why I'm here for the rules of the fight."

Will arose from his chair and faced Garth. "So this is what its all about...to tell who's the better man in a fight"

"Precisely."

"Well, I'm not interested. My capabilities are well known and I don't have to go around proving them to anyone, in spite of what I'm supposed to have told you."

Garth again lashed his cruel smile.

"But you have to, Marshal. The word's gotten out in the fight world. Bets are being laid on it. Some say you can't take our man in a fair fight."

Will stopped short. Then it came back to him, Earlier he had agreed to this fight. But that was before he was really content with his full capabilities. But he can't show a yellow flag on this.

He sighed. "Alright, Garth. Now I remember. I did agree to this match so I can't back down and show any cowardice. We'll meet at my training lot next week from today. "

"Don't worry." Garth said. "All will be provided and I want permission to place chairs on the lot."

"Fine. You've got it."

"Believe me, Garth continued. "This will be a fight of the century, as it were. A lot of people are aware of this."

Will frowned. "Don't turn this into a circus, Garth." .

"Worry not about it. We won't. Marshal." He exited.

"You did what?" Later, Margaret was ostensibly upset about the news from Will at home when Arthur was present.

"I have to, Margy," A lot is riding on this fight, including money.

"Why do you have to fight this man? Why must you prove yourself? We know who you are."

"But not all know it," Will replied. "Garth and his men have alerted newspapers and lots of reporters will be there."

"Do you think you can take him, Will?" Arthur said. "This man Groat has a reputation as a top boxer and has won many fights."

"I know that," Will replied. "But I'm confident with my capabilities and that's what counts. I must prove---to the whole world if necessary--- that I can take on and defeat a professional boxer and I'm ready to prove it."

Margaret exhaled her breath, with a modicum of disgust. "You men and your pride. Well, if you must you must. I know you, Will Howard and I know those capabilities of which you speak and I know you're a man of his word. My only prayer will be that you won't be hurt."

"I don't expect to be," Will answered.

"Then so be it," Arthur said. "Will won't disappoint us."

"I've been trained to handle such a situation" Will answered, a determine look on his face. "There'll be no more argumentation."

The next day, Will was at his office going through one of the volumes of wanted posters he received.

"You're doing well, Will. You haven't disappointed me."

Will glanced up. It was Kim Lee again standing there smiling softly. He'd come from nowhere.

Will glanced around. "Kim Lee, Where'd you come from?"

"We won't discuss that now. Just say that you need help and I responded."

Will shook his head in disbelieve. "Someday you'll tell me how you do it. But for now I'm glad you're here and I do need you."

"I know your situation," Kim replied. "I'm ready to help. May we go to your training lot?"

"Of course," Will responded. "Mark will take over here. I'll get into my dobok, and meet you there."

Later at the lot, Will was in his uniform, while Kim was clad in a dubok containing many symbols and a black belt. Will was impressed; full of questions, but he decided to hold his peace for a time.

"Now remember, Will. This man is a boxer. I was fortunate once to see him in a fight and studied his technique. He is a brawler and slugger. He'll try to get you close in, by using short jabs. when you're in close range he'll try to finish you off with a straight hook or an uppercut. It's standard strategy with boxers. keep him close in, jab him, then deliver a decisive blow.

"He'll try to keep you close. Kim replied, "There are some counter moves I'll reach you. Your task will be to avoid getting those jabs and hard punches."

"I'm all ears," Will said, facetiously. "Carry on, Macduff."

"You and your Shakespeare," "Kim replied, laughing. "Now let us get started."

Kim put him through a vigorous round of defense techniques, Tang Soo Do-style. When they had finished to Kim's satisfaction, he bowed and said, "I have taught you all I know about defense moves. They should do you well. I don't know about any matches between a boxer and a martial arts expert, but I am satisfied you will hold your own against this fist-fighter. Now I must go, but you will see me again. Good bye, my friend."

Will extended his hand for a shake, but remembered it wasn't the oriental tradition. He snapped to attention and bowed. Kim responded with the same.

Both changed from uniforms to regular clothing. As they were ready to depart, Kim faced Will and took him by the shoulders.

"Just remember the most important things I have taught you. Believe in yourself and your abilities and don't allow anyone to change your goals or beliefs. You have been an unexceptional student and have learned well. Now take what I have taught you and use it decisively."

Will started to leave, but Kim stopped him.

"I leave you with the saying by Sun Tzu Lu in his Art of War: 'He will win who has properly prepared himself to confront his opponent'" I will see you again."

He turned and again with unbelievable swiftness, departed.. Will stood, watching after him. "My friend. I do hope we meet again."

For a time, he pondered the impenetrable mystery aura that always seems to be around Kim Lee, but the black belt told him much. Then he sighed, shrugged and added: "Who or whatever you really are, my friend."

He turned his attention to the task of changing clothes. He took his dubok, carefully folded it and placed it in a hand bag Kim had given him. He headed back to his office.

Once there he found Mark busy sorting a new batch of wanted posters. Mark looked at him, with a growing interest. "I know that it's none of my business, but were you learning from that Kim Lee about the coming fight?"

Will stared at him for a beat. "How did you know about--?" He paused and, with a serious face, stared intently at Mark who shrugged and took on an innocent face.

"Well, Mark, I'm not surprised you knew about I hoped to keep it secret, but now the whole world seems to know about my training program with Kim Lee."

"Yes, Marshal. It's common knowledge."

"True. It's an ancient system of fighting by the Koreans and was the only way they defended themselves against the soldiers of the tyrannical armies. They used the only weapons they had, their hands and feet."

Mark chuckled. "I guess I'll never understand some of the words you use, but they do make good sense. But I will say this: that system, as you call it, is certainly the right way of defending oneself."

He studied Will a moment before continuing. "You said you would teach me some of that, remember?"

Will smiled. "Yes, of course. I remember. And I'll be happy to teach you. We'll find a hole in our schedules and do it."

Mark beamed with pleasure. "Thanks, Marshal. I'd really appreciate that."

"I'm going home for a while to check on things. Take over."

"Sure, thing, Marshal."

With a puzzled sigh, Will left the room, leaving Mark to ponder it all that happened.

Margaret was up and around, looking more comforted since her recent troubles, when Will arrived, especially about losing her child. He knew

Tommy was at school. He kissed her and together they sat and sipped hot coffee.

"I've reconciled myself to the loss, Will. It'll be a while healing over it. But I'm concerned over this fight."

"Why? Certainly you aren't worried he may beat me."

"No. It's just the thought that the only way to resolve a problem is to fight it out and may the best man win. It seems to be the way the world thinks."

"Margie," Will responded. "There is always a rule of honor between men, through the ages. I know it date back to dueling days in history, but it has always been with us through history.

You're always quoting Shakespeare. The play "Hamlet' seems to be tinged with echoes of honor. Quote: 'lay on, Macduff and may the best man win.' That's a case of honor."

He put his arm around her. "This is a case of honor, in a way. I have to prove that defiance of the law must be met, either by talk, the gun or the fist. Otherwise there'll be anarchy and you know how destructive that can be,"

"I agree to an extent," Margaret replied. "Your honor and your service to the community has been challenged. I grant you that. But why through more violence?"

He laughed. "Do you in your wildest dreams think that talking to a man like Groat and his sycophants would change them change from their ways and make them model citizens?"

She got to her feet and faced him. "Let's leave the philosophy of violence versus. the community to experts. And enjoy the time we have together. I'll fine, I had the best teacher in the world for self-defense,"

What is it about Kim Lee, Will? When is all said and done, what do you really know about him?"

He comes and goes most mysteriously. We know nothing about his life.

"I can't answer that positively Margie," Will answered. "And I was sure you would ask me again. There's no doubt he is a very unusual man. He seems to know things I've never heard of or knew about. He always seems to show up at the right moment and have an answer to what's troubling me."

Her face took on a sheepish look. "You don't think, in your wildest seams that perhaps he's—he's an angel or something? You were a clergyman at one time and that's why I thought you'd have a clue about that possibility."

Will looked down at his feet and began to make motions as if scraping away something invisible. "I'm afraid I don't have a clue, Dear. I know the Bible tells about angels taking on human form at times, but that was usually something for the fulfillment of God's plans. I don't think Kim fits that criteria."

"Then what is it?"

"I believe he's a man with very sensitive and far-reaching thoughts on things we don't know enough about. As for a supernatural being I'm not so sure, even though at times it appears so. He's an enigma for sure and I'm not ready to reach any final conclusion."

He got to his feet and prepared to leave. "As for a rational answer I'm not so sure. Maybe there is and it sometimes seems so. But for now let's be grateful he's our friend."

She sighed. "Of course you're right as usual."

She kissing him on the cheek." Now vamoose back to your duties."

"Right as usual, my dear." he reached for his Stetson on the deer antler hat rack, left and headed straight for his office.

Duties were waiting when Will arrived back at the office. Even with recent events, the constant pressures of his office and the coming fight, he plunged into some paper work piled up on his desk. "Look at this mess. i wish I could afford a secretary now and then."

He was thus engaged when the door opened and a man entered, a briefcase under his arm. He was tall, white-haired and wearing a well-pressed suit. He peered out through a pair of wire-rimmed spectacles.

"Marshal Howard?" His voice was strong and well-modulated.

Will looked him over very quickly and then nodded. "I'm Marshal Howard. What can I do for you?"

"Permit me to introduce myself." The man answered. I am Phineas Quinn. "Here's my card."

He handed Will a card. "As you will see I am a promoter of public events, including that of fights."

The card was embossed in large gold letters. He studied it for a moment.

"'Phineas P. Quinn, promoter and sponsor of public events'? He read aloud. "You've come a long way from St. Louis," He said to Quinn. "I trust this is about the fight."

Quinn opened his briefcase and arranged papers on the desk.

"Yes, Sir, it is. May I sit here while we talk?"

"Certainly," Will replied, moving a chair alongside his.

Quinn removed a handkerchief from his side pocket and proceeded to brush the seat off before he sat down. Slightly amused, Will watched him, his mind whirling with expectation. He surmised that it was obviously very important if this well-to-do person came all the way from St. Louis to see him about something.

"Now, Mr. Quinn, what can I do for you?" he said.

"My mission is simple," Quinn replied. "My client has formally challenged you to a fight to the finish to be held at a place already chosen and no Queensbury rules to apply. It will be held without any provisions whatsoever."

As he spoke, he glanced around the office, with obvious disdain on his face.

"So that's it." Will said. "This fight is to be a grandstand event complete with crowds and bands, instead of a mere fight."

Quinn blinked at him through his spectacles. "Oh yes, Marshal. Official publicity will be held, but will not be a 'grandstand event,' as you put it."

Will gave a soft laugh. "Forgive me, Mr. Quinn, but I have never been 'officially' challenged to a fight before. Why all this formality? Who is your client and why isn't with you? Shouldn't he be here?" Where is the one called "Garth?"

"I don't know. I never question the motives of my clients. Quinn said. "I merely do what they want. Now what is your answer? Will you sign this or not?"

"I know I'm fighting someone called 'Groat' Who is he?"

"I'm not at liberty to reveal information about my client, Marshal. You should know that. As for your opponent, you have it right. Mr. Groat, as I can reveal, is a known prizefighter with many wins to his credit. In the fight game he's known as 'The Mauler.'"

"What does he know about me?" Will was becoming a bit wary as the conversation proceeded. "Does he know I'm not a prizefighter?"

"He knows that and he knows about your conversion from traditional fist fighting to the Oriental method. That is why he's most anxious to fight you and prove that a traditional boxer can defeat such a fighter."

Now I was all clear to Will. "So that's it. A situation of honor. The new versus the old."

"I beg your pardon,"

"Never mind, Mr. Quinn. You tell your client that I will meet this Groat person in the ring as planned and not just to prove who is the better fighter." Will said. "Also tell him I'm not doing this just to gamble my reputation over a mere challenge. Do you understand that? As for the Queensbury rules. I don't care which rules apply. It's to be a mere fight."

Blinking a bit behind his spectacles, Quinn nodded his head. "I will do just that, Marshal. And tt will be a regular fight. Nothing special."

"Agreed." Will replied. "Tell the promoters I'll meet him Next week on Wednesday, as planned, at nine in the morning at the vacant lot where we have plenty of room for spectators."

Quinn's blinking increased with his obvious nervousness over the situation. "Very well. I'll inform my client."

"Thank you," Will replied, with a bit of sarcasm in his voice. "Now if you will excuse me, I have some government business to attend to."

Quinn made some notes in a small, black-cover book and replaced it in his vest pocket. "Very well. We will see you there."

He left the office. Will sat staring after him for a few beats. "I only hope I'm doing the right thing," he said to himself. Then he turned his attention back to his desk.

When he returned home, he told Margaret about his talk with Quinn and about the agreements.

"You agreed to what?" Margaret's face was intense with disbelief. "Explain yourself to me."

Will looked at her, with incredulity. "What was I to do? I was challenged. I must respond. I couldn't refuse a challenge, because it smacks of cowardice. You know that it's been the way of the frontier and will always be so."

"I don't care about the rules of the frontier," Margaret replied, her anger growing. "You're the U.S. Marshal of a city. You have a wife and son. You're liable to be badly hurt, or what's worse, killed. How can you risk that in a mere circus?"

Will tempered his feelings a bit. He took her by the shoulders and faced her squarely. "Look, it's not merely a case if loosing respect as a lawman or looking like a man in the face of a challenge. It's a thing that defies rules and morays. If I am to go on being respected as The Fighting Marshal, a fearless lawman in he eyes of lawbreakers, I must meet this challenge."

He paused to let his words sink in." How can I allow that to be destroyed by refusing one fight? I had many of them, and it didn't bother you. Why this one?"

Her temper flared again. "Bother me? Is that how you look at it. I am your wife and mother and I see you in real danger this time."

"Why? He's just another man, just another thug to me."

"He's a professional boxer, a skilled fighter. You've never faced anyone like him before. He may seriously hurt you."

"No, dear, you underestimate me. Kim has taught me well. He knows about this and gives his approval. He's confident I can beat this Groat person, no matter how good he is as a boxer." He paused, took a deep breath: "No, it's settled. I'll fight him, circus or no circus, without much harm to myself. I guarantee you that much."

Margaret backed away and studied his face. "You're dead serious about this, aren't you? You'll defend your honor and reputation at all costs. Am I right about this, Will Howard?"

"Yes. That's the way it is. "I will  defend my hard-earned reputation."

He turned and walked away, leaving a much-disturbed Margaret behind, staring after him. "Of course you'll do as your heart dictates. You always do. But I only pray you'll come through this unscathed."

William Groat came to town the next day.

He was accompanied by his trainer, Cyrus Mann, Quinn and a flat-nosed individual known only as "Hank" whose duties weren't made clear. Individuals in the lobby at the time caught a glimpse of the celebrated prizefighter. He was tall, well-proportioned and many women concluded he was rather handsome.

"Where's your fighter?" Cyrus Mann exclaimed, looking around, openly ignoring the stares of the patrons.

"He's making his rounds," the clerk nervously explained, looking over the entourage.

Rounds? What are they?" Groat replied." Never heard of them, except for bullets."

"As a United States marshal he's required to walk around the town, checking everything at least once a day, but mostly two."

"I never fought a U.S. marshal before, especially one trained in some sort of slant-eyed style of fighting." said Groat. 'Now I must go to my dressing room and rest up," He added. "Tell that lawman fighter I'm ready to meet him. Cyrus, take care of things."

"Sure thing, Boss," Cyrus said. Meanwhile, Hank set about gathering the many pieces of luggage around.

"I'll inform the marshal you're here," the clerk said.

"He's here and ready to meet me?" Will replied, when informed by a boy sent to give him the message at his office.

"Yes, Sir," the boy replied. "What shall I tell him, Sir?"

"Tell him I'll be there in—" he checked his pocket watch--"two hours from now."

"Yes, Sir," the boy turned to leave, but hesitated and turned to Will. "Ain't my place to say so, Marshal, but I seen this guy and gave him the eye. I sure think you'll take him."

Will smiled at him. 'Thank you, Jimmy. I appreciate your confidence."

After Jimmy left, Will prepared to get ready for the event by getting into his dubok.

He was thus unpacking his uniform, when Margaret and Tommy came in. She glanced at him and then at the uniform. "So you're going to go through with it?"

"Can't help it, Margie," My authority has been questioned and I must respond. I have no choice, otherwise I'll never hold up my head in this town again. Besides, half the town's population said they'd be there."

Margaret sighed. "I know. I've been thinking about it and I realize the position you're in. You men put so much faith in your unwritten masculine laws. There's no use arguing you out of it."

He came over and hugged both of them.. "Don't worry. I'll do the best I can and, after what I've learned from Kim Lee, I think I have a good chance against this prizefighter, even if it's never been defeated before. You two don't have to be there to watch."

"We'll be rooting you, Dad," Tommy said. "I know you can take him."

They hugged once, twice. Then she turned and left, wiping her eyes. Will watched them go. Then he looked skyward. "Lord, it's been a long time since I've talked with you. I know I've walked away from the ministry, but you know I love and trust you always. All I ask is for you to be with me. This is more than just a fight; it's a case of defending principles of honor."

The day came and To Will's disappointment, the area was crowded with spectators. He turned to Mark who met him at the door. "Can't help it, Marshal. That promotion person had invited them and I couldn't stop them from coming in. That rough buzzard kept us out and I didn't want to call his bluff."

"It's no bluff, Mark. You did right."

The combat area was Spartan—a single mat on the floor and a table with a few chairs. The few onlookers allowed to be in were crowded around the arena. Looking around, Will noticed that Cyrus Mann and his entourage were nowhere in sight.

"Where's my opponent?" Will said. "Did he change his mind?"

"Knock him into the next county, Marshal!" someone shouted.

"Yea, change his face," another shouted."

"Where the hell is he?' Sill another shouted.

"He's a'comin," someone near a window shouted. Wait til you see 'im. Looks like a circus performer, he does."

As if in answer to all of this, the door flew open and Groat and his handlers came in. The crowd issued a few half-hearted cheers; Will surmised they were panted in the crowd. "What arrogance," he muttered to Mark Groat, in a bright blue robe, responded by raising his clapped hands over his head in a boxer's salute. He looked around and his gaze fixed on Will and Mark. "Where's your handlers??"

Will pointed at Mark. "He's it. Don't need an entourage."

"Correction. you got one," The voice came from the back of the room

All eyes turned in that direction as a small man stepped forward. Will gasped. It was Kim Lee. He was clad in a bright white dubok with a large black belt tied around his waist.

Will said, "I'm glad to see you again."

"You didn't think I'd miss this, did you? My prize student?"

"Who the hell's this? What student?" Cyrus said. "Don't know anything about a 'student.'".

"Meet Master Kim Lee my trainer," Will said

"So he's the one who taught you that Chinee kind of fighting?.."

Kim flashed that inscrutable smile of his. "Yes. It was my pleasure to train him in Tung Soo Do. And I'm Korean, not 'Chinee' as you put it."

"Don't matter," Groat said. "I'll show you that a good boxer kin beat any kind of fighting—Korean, Jap, Chink or whatever."

"Forget all that," Cyrus Mann said, "Just remember that a fight's a fight and the Queensbury Rules don't apply here. The fight ends when one's down and out."

Groat removed his robe and stepped to the middle of the mat.

He was clad in what resembled long underwear or "long Johns."

Bright's gaze swept over Will's dubok "Never seen anythin' like it. What in hell is that outfit's for?"

"Korean fighters wear it in combat," Kim explained.

"Don't matter much," Groat replied, blood'll be spilt on it before long."

"If you two are ready, I'll start when I fire my pistol." Bright said, raising a pistol in the air. .

Groat took a boxer's stance: leg's slightly apart, knees slightly bent. His left fist was close to his head, while the right was extended out, elbows bent.

Will's stance was different; His feet were apart and his body was also a 45-degree angle. He shifted his weight to the left leg while his right leg was at a forty-five degree angle. His right arm was across his chest while his left was slightly above waist level Both fists were tightly closed. Groat and his handlers exchanged glances. They'd never seen a fighting stance like this before.

Cyrus fired the pistol and they started sparring.

Groat stood straight and began a typical boxer's stance a weaving movement, with fists in a rotating movement.

Will stood ready, his eyes watching Groat's every move.

Suddenly Groat threw a quick jab, but it missed as Will deftly stepped aside. Then Groat resumed his dance-like moves, with Will still standing still, watching his opponent's every move. Groat's right fist shot out, but missed again. Then he started to circle.

As he crossed in front of him, Will suddenly bent at waist level, his left leg shot out, curved and slammed into Groat's shin.

Groat howled with pain and did a crooked dance a way from his opponent. He kept watching Will closely, as did Cyrus Mann and his handlers whose mouths were wide open in astonishment.

Both fighters assumed their stances. This time Groat was more wary of Will's movements. Will's stance had changed. he kept his fists now at waist level, a move that puzzled his handlers and they exchanged glances. The men sparred around the ring, neither one throwing any punches. It was obvious that Groat wasn't as sure of himself as he did at the beginning of the match.

Will's stance changed. Now he was keeping his fists at waist. level. His opponent and handlers were openly puzzled by this change in stance.

"He's like a goddam sidewinder," Groat muttered, keeping a wary eye on his opponent.

Suddenly, one of Groat's lightening-like jabs connected. Will stepped back, slightly surprised and dazed from the heaviness of the punch. He shook his head to clear it. Groat, seeing this, stepped in to land another punch. He had lost some of his wariness now and was moving in to deliver a decisive punch, He threw a punch, but Will deftly stepped aside and as it went by, he grabbed Groat's arm raised it high over his head and twisted it downward. Groat was forced to bend down. With his other open hand, Will landed a knife-like slash on the back of Groat's neck. It was a swift and powerful blow.

As Groat bent forward from the blow, Will heaved upward on the arm, whirled and Groat did a summersault and slammed to the mat.

The crowd howled their approval and excitement at this spectacle they had never before seen.

Howling with pain, Groat lay on the mat, dazed with his hand on his shoulder.

Will stepped back and assumed his fighting stance.

But Groat wasn't through yet. Amazingly, he scrambled to his feet, head shaking off dizziness and pain. He assumed his fighting stance, bringing a slight groan from the spectators.

Both fighters started sparring again. This time, Groat was far more wary of his opponent. He glanced at Cyrus for some kind of response. Cyrus grimaced and raised a clenched fist, giving the signal for the kill. Will was holding his fighting stance, ready to spring into action.

Groat started another series of fast jabs, hoping to force Will off his guard. One landed and Will staggered a bit. He landed another punch that gazed Will's head.

Then Groat bent slightly to land a decisive punch. Will swiftly raised his right leg and landed a snap-kick to Groat's head, stopping him cold.

Groat stepped back, dazed by the ferocity of the kick. "Damn it!"

Will glanced over at Kim who merely nodded his head slightly.

Taking advantage of his opponent's open weakness, Will suddenly leaped high in the air, spun around and delivered a straight, powerful kick to Groat's head, snapping it back and slamming him to the mat where he lay helpless, dazed and bleeding. It was obvious to everyone he had been beaten for good by a most unorthodox method of fighting they had ever witnessed.

The spectators went berserk, howling and clapping. Groat's handlers moved in to assist their beaten fighter, while Will's backers swarmed into the makeshift ring, raising his arm in a victory salute.

Will looked around for Kim lee, but he couldn't find that worthy. He turned to greet a man who had approached to give congratulations. When he turned again, Kim was standing there, smiling at him.

"How di you di it, Kim? You were nowhere and suddenly here and now. I'll never figure it out."

Kim smiled. "A moot point. The main fact is you did very well. That final  spin kick was as flawless as I've ever seen it."

"Thanks to you," Will replied.

"Remember, my friend, I will always be with you and at your command." Kim said. "Soon you'll be a Tang Soo Do Master."

Before Will could answer, he was joggled by an  excited admirer and was temporarily distracted. When he turned back,  Kim was gone. "Damn it! How does he do that?  The  man's a magician."  He decided to get out of there and see Margaret. As he walked out, an admirer shouted: "Three cheers for the world's champion fighting marshal!  Right here for all

When he reached the door, Cyrus Mann blocked his way. The two men stood, staring hard at each other.

Will was starting to think he might have to fight his way past Groat's entourage, when, to his surprise, Mann smiled and extended his hand. "I congratulate you on a fair fight. You've shown that a man trained in that so-called Tung Soo thing can not only hold his way against a trained boxer but beat him in a fair fight."

Will smiled and shook his hand. "Tell, Mr. Groat I'm sorry to have hurt him. He'll recover and hopefully appreciate other kinds of fighting. At least I think he has a good impression of  oriental fighting techniques and will respect them"

"Oh, I know he will," Cyrus said. "He'll have the scars and pains from it for a while. But we must not forget that even although I beat Groat who is a skilled fighter doesn't mean it may someday happen. Nothing in sports is  etched in stone."

"I will remember that," Tommy replied.

Then Margaret and Tommy met Will as he walked into the house and they hugged him.

"You were great, dad, added Tommy. "You showed him what it's like to be a real fighter."

"I was so worried about you." Margaret touched the bruises on his face. "Do they hurt? I was afraid you were hit hard by that brute a few times"

"They don't bother me much. I expected much worse."

"I was really proud of you, Dad," Tommy said. "I told all my friends that you are the greatest marshal in all the west."

"That's the best part of my victory," Will replied. "Come here son."

Tommy came to him and they hugged. "You're my man to carry on Tommy."

As expected, the Howard victory caused a real stir in the Dodge City community. Congratulations were offered from everywhere, in person, mail and notes left on the doorstep. Even the Wichita newspapers carried stories of the fight and other papers in the west picked up on them, It solidified Will's reputation as the one and only "Fighting Marshal."

Meanwhile, Groat and his entourage left town, with all still puzzled and amazed by the fighting expertise of Will Howard, and they weren't about to forget it soon.

A party was planned and executed by Margaret, Lucy and others in the community. It was crowded with friends and admirers.

Afterwards, Margaret, Will and Tommy, wanting to be alone for a while, stole away to their house.

"Margie, Tommy, I could never be where we are without you," Will said.

He pulled them to him and they hugging each other.

"What now?' she said.

"We'll continue on," Will replied. "The future looks promising for us and my legacy will be established for Tommy to carry on ."

Will's legacy, as he predicted, seemed to be assured, Kansas papers and even Chicago's editions, lauded the fight and "the most unorthodox fight in ring history." Some questioned that statement, but, nevertheless, no one stepped forward to prove otherwise.

When questioned, Will replied, "The one thing I learned is there is never only one way of doing things." We all can learn from that."

And, of course, there were those around who didn't accept the Howard legacy and mystique and refused to agree with it.

But then that's another story yet to be told.

## THE END